SOUTHERN ROOTS

J. MORGAN

For all my cliff jumpers, and those who dare to dream big.

CHAPTER 1

"*H*ey Rob, you got mail, man." His roommate called across the dorm room.

Robert pressed his laptop spacebar and the screen came to life. He nodded, "Thanks; leave it on my table." He glanced over at his roommate, who had just stepped out of the shower, towel wrapped around his waist. Bruises from last night's wrestling match were already evident on his abdomen. "Dude, you all right? Shit looks like it hurts."

"What this? Hell yeah, I'm good. I fucking won, man!" He slapped his abs then groaned through gritted teeth. "Totally worth it."

Robert chuckled. "Yeah, I see that." He smirked then turned back to his laptop. After opening his email, his brows raised in shock. "Wedding ceremony?"

"You getting married, fucker?" His roommate chuckled then wandered back into the bathroom.

He ignored him and opened the email.

Bobby Ray,

I'm getting married kiddo. I'd love it if you would be my best man. Consider it; I can't imagine anyone else doing it. You'll receive a formal invite from Sabrina here soon. You remember her; she's been with me for quite a while. Figured if she can put up with your old man this long, might as well make it permanent. That and I love her. Soon we'll be Mr. and Mrs. Shaw. I miss you a lot, son. I'm looking forward to having you here for the summer.

Love you,

Dad (and Sabrina)

Robert smiled as he read the letter. "Damn, Dad's getting married." He thought back to when his mother had left his father. He remembered his old man growing smaller and smaller as he watched him out the back window of his mother's car. He was ten when they divorced. His mother packed up and moved to Georgia. Eventually, she married into money, which was what she had always wanted anyway. "I wonder if she knows," he thought aloud.

He looked at the calendar hanging on the wall beside him, then back to the wedding invite. "An August wedding. You gotta be kidding me, Dad. It'll be damn hot!" He shook his head and looked back at the calendar again. Classes ended on June first then he started his senior year.

"Hell, I'm going back to Texas." He sighed and pressed reply. *"Can't wait, see you and Sabrina soon. Of course, I'll be your best man. I can't imagine Old Man Cooter standing up there in his overalls. Tell Sabrina she's making a mistake and to run off with the younger version of you."* He chuckled then pressed send. He thought his soon-to-be stepmother was good looking for her age, but he would never consider her a cougar. The thought made him shudder.

Robert grabbed his phone and sighed as he pressed the speed dial button. He listened to the phone ring until she picked up. "Hey honey. Is everything okay? How are classes?"

"Hey, Mom. Yeah, I'm good. Listen, I need to tell you something and I'd rather you hear it from me first."

"What, that your father's getting re-married? Yeah, I already know."

"Really? How?" He relaxed, thankful he didn't have to break the news that his old man had finally moved on.

"Being married to the Senator has its perks, you know." He imagined she was smiling into the phone. "I get tabs on him occasionally when he does something... outrageous."

"Dad getting married is outrageous?" Robert reached up and rubbed the back of his neck.

"Well, no, not exactly. Just in this position, there's power. Where there's power..."

He cut her off, "Yeah there's responsibility to those who may affect you. Yep, got it."

"So, you're going I take it?"

"Yeah, why wouldn't I?"

"Oh no, I didn't mean it like that, honey. I'm glad you're going. I hope his new wife can give him everything I couldn't."

Robert rolled his eyes. "Sure, Mom, whatever you say. I'll be leaving some time after school lets out. Tell Dad, would you? I might be able to catch up with a few of the professors out in Texas, you know, get a feel for the law out there." His stepfather, Rick, had entered his mother's life when Robert was barely eleven and he had never left. Rick had been very good to his mother, and Robert had instantly felt at home with him. He would never take the place of his father, but Robert knew he had someone he could look up to... and trust. Rick treated him as if he were his own son.

"I sure will, honey. I'll tell him as soon as he gets home. And honey," she stopped talking for a moment, as if considering her words.

"Yeah, Mom?"

"Watch out for the women there. If they know who your stepfather is... well they may come after you for the wrong reasons."

"Oh, like it's any different here?"

She let a soft laugh escape. "Exactly. Just be safe and when you get there, do let me know." She could hear the reluctance in his voice and continued. "Robert, you're still my damn son. Call or text me when you get there; that's all I'm asking."

He groaned into the phone. "Damn, you make me feel like a kid. Fine, I'll do it. Anything else?"

"You'll always be my little boy, Robert. You'll know that feeling one day when you have children of your own. Oh, and that had better be a long way from now! I'm too young to be a grandmother."

He chuckled. "Yes, ma'am. I love you, Mom."

"I love you, too."

"Aww, I love you, too, Mrs. McAlister!" His roommate called across the room.

"Dude, seriously? This is my mom!" Robert hissed at his roommate.

She giggled into the phone. "You tell Ben I miss his smile! Okay honey, talk to you soon. Bye." She hung up and Robert set his phone down.

"Classy, you fucker. That's my mom."

"Yeah, and she's a cougar! Fucking hot!" Ben chuckled then dodged a baseball thrown at his head. "You need to work on your throw." He chuckled again then walked out of the dorm room, a cloud of cologne in his wake.

Robert fanned the air in front of him. "Fucker."

～

The plane sped down the runway; Robert leaned back, and relaxed in his first class seat. He glanced out his window and watched the earth pull farther and farther away. The sound of the pilot allowing the passengers to leave their seats echoed throughout the cabin.

"You may now use appropriate airline approved electronics. Please refer to your safety guide for permitted devices. Enjoy your flight."

Robert tuned him out, pushed his ear buds in, and turned on his iPod. His playlist kicked in as he relaxed deeper into his seat. At a soft tap on his shoulder, he looked at a smiling flight attendant, offering drinks, a cold towel, and anything else he would like.

He accepted the coke and asked for a bottle of Captain's. The flight attendant, whose name badge read Sally, handed it over and kept smiling and blushing. His hand barely touched hers and he thought she would jump out of her skin.

"Is everything okay?" He asked her.

"Yes, sir, it sure is!" She smiled and grabbed her cart, then turned back. "Are you, Senator McAlister's son? You seem very familiar."

"Yes, ma'am, well stepson, but yes." He nodded at Sally and she giggled.

"Well, Mr. McAlister, if there's anything else I can get for you, anything at all…" She trailed off and smiled.

"It's actually Shaw. McAlister is my stepfather's name." He smiled then went back to his iPod. At times, he considered not correcting them and allowing the people he met to call him McAlister. Then again, he was a Shaw. He loved his stepfather but he would never take his name.

Sally said a few other things to him, but he blocked her out of his mind. His music played and he pulled out a law book he'd brought for the flight. He flipped it open and began reading laws protecting family rights, property, and dwellings. He'd had to pick an area of law to study and felt fortunate he'd picked family law.

Soon, the plane began to descend and he watched Sally pass by once more. If he were a betting man, he thought he could join the Mile High Club with her. She probably wouldn't put up much of a fight about it, aside from making room in the small bathroom. Hell, you could barely stand in that small excuse of a pisser. He caught her eye and she smiled, then he thought back to something his stepfather had said.

"Don't do anything that could jeopardize you, me, or the family. Other than that, tear shit up." Robert had chuckled with his stepfather, shook his hand before he hugged him. He really did look up to the man.

The plane landed safely and, as Robert walked past the attendant, she slipped her number into his hand. He winked at her and went to pocket it. As soon as he walked down the tarmac, he tossed it into the nearby trashcan. If a woman was this easy, there's no telling who else she gave her shit to. No, thanks.

He grabbed his luggage off the turnstile and looked around. Cowboy hats, baseball caps, boots, jeans... *shit were those spurs?* He thought to himself. Yeah, he was in Texas. He smirked and turned to walk toward passenger pick-up, when a sign caught his attention. In big, bold, bright pink letters against a florescent yellow poster board, read the following passage:

BOBBY RAY, YOU SAID IF I STAND HERE LONG ENOUGH WITH THIS SIGN, THE CRAZY PEOPLE WILL FIND ME. APPARENTLY, I'M TOO CRAZY FOR THEIR LIKING!

He chuckled and shook his head. His cousin, Makayla, never missed a beat. She was always ready and willing to give a jab when he needed it. He walked up to her and watched as she pretended not to notice him.

"Bobby Ray! Bobby Ray, where are you?" She tried not to laugh and even snorted a few times.

"Put that fucking sign down, cuz and gimme a hug!" He snatched the awful sign from her grasp and pulled her in close.

"HELP! Don't touch me like you know me!"

People stopped to look at them and Robert pulled away from her. "What the hell is wrong with you?"

She busted out laughing to the point she bent over and grabbed her thigh. "Ahh hell, Bobby Ray! I haven't seen you in years! You haven't changed at all!"

"Bitch, last time you saw me I was fifteen years old! I've not changed?" He raised a brow.

She righted herself. "Okay, so you changed... a little." She pressed her fingers close together. "Like, this much."

He shook his head. "You haven't changed at all; except you got tits. Damn, you grew up."

"Gross! Stop staring! Perv!"

He laughed a hard belly laugh. "Right, that's me, the perv. C'mon, let's go. Dad know I landed yet?"

"Yeah I called him and Aunt Sabrina to let them know you're here."

Her calling his soon-to-be stepmom Aunt didn't go unnoticed. "So... she's good for Pop?"

"Yeah, she's really nice. She's been really good for him. And Bobby Ray," she paused and looked up at him. "He's really happy. You know your dad was really upset when your mom left him."

He nodded. "Yeah, I know. Trust me. I heard all the time how disappointed she was in herself for remaining with him as long as she did." Makayla shook her head as they headed toward the door. "You know, Rick is a great guy. He leveled her out... so to speak."

"With what? His wit or money?"

Robert chuckled. "Exactly." She smiled as they approached a new Chevy Tundra. The truck was an extended cab and dark maroon in color. "Damn cuz, you did well for yourself."

"Thank you." She smiled and pressed the unlock button on her key chain. "Get in, you get to ride bitch!" She giggled and opened her door as Robert tossed his luggage into the back.

"I should grab the keys right now and make you ride bitch!"

The two laughed when she started up the truck. She swiped her hand across the dashboard. "I love my Sassy Thing."

"Sassy thing?" He questioned.

"Yes, Sassy Thing. That's her name. Be good to my baby."

Robert chuckled. "Sure, just... please, call me Robert. No more Bobby Ray. I haven't gone by that name in years."

"Well, you're gonna have to get used to it, *Bobby Ray*." She purposely over enunciated his name with a grin. "Everyone is coming out to tonight's bonfire party. There are people coming who haven't seen you in a long time. Some are calling it a reunion; a chance to get out and party."

"Nice. It'll be nice to have a cold beer, a hot chick on my lap, and maybe go for some diving."

"You remember the cliffs?" She smiled and pulled out onto the interstate.

"Hell yeah, I do! Best part of the damn summers here was jumping off those damn cliffs!"

The conversation went on for a while until silence filled the cab. She reached over and turned up the music. Robert found himself looking out the window, having no idea what country artist was playing on the radio.

She looked over with a grin. "Do you feel like you walked into a foreign country?"

He looked over at his cousin. "Am I that obvious?" She nodded. "Well, I seldom listen to country these days. I've not been to a rodeo since... hell, since I was I think 15. Last time I rode a horse was at Pop's. Yeah, I feel like the outsider here."

"Don't worry about it. Everything will come back quickly. Even your accent."

"My accent? What the hell is wrong with my accent?"

"You sound as if you lost it. Like... northern or some shit."

He chuckled. "I moved to Georgia, not the north east."

"Right, but you know anything north of Dallas is Yankee."

"So you keep telling me on Facebook. Nice, cuz."

She grinned and lightly punched his arm. "Welcome home, Robert." He looked at her with appreciation. "And that's the last time I'm calling you that name. You are, and forever will be, Bobby Ray."

"Outstanding." He shook his head and looked back out the window.

Makayla pulled off the interstate and took the main strip out of town, toward the country. He looked around and found where forests of trees once stood had been plowed and made into strip malls, outparcels and gas stations. "Pop still have the farm?"

"Yup."

"That's cool." About half an hour off the main road, Makayla pulled down the long dirt road that led to his father's home. Lights surrounding the wrap around front porch were lit up from the commotion of the dogs. They came running toward Makayla's truck, barking loudly. "Hell, how many does he have?"

"Well, that depends on what you call his."

"What do you mean?"

"He's breeding English Pointers. The others are just strays he feeds." She put the truck into park and turned it off. "Don't worry, they're all nice."

"Oh, that's good to know."

She grinned. "Once they smell your crotch."

"What? Uff!" Almost knocked back when a few noses found their way between his legs, he said, "Alright now, back off, that's enough of the formal greeting." He pushed the dogs back as they barked and wagged their tails. He closed the truck door then reached for his luggage. "Pop here?"

"Yeah I think so. UNCLE JIM! BOBBY RAY'S HERE!" Makayla yelled out as loud as she could.

Robert shook his head. "I see pig calling lessons came in handy."

"I have never pig called, you asshole." She rolled her eyes and walked toward the front of the house.

He chuckled and followed her toward the porch. The front door opened and there stood Robert's image on an older man. He had always been told he looked just like his father.

James Shaw still had a head full of hair and Robert was happy to see that. His father smiled then walked out onto the porch, extending his arms. "C'mere boy! Come give your old man a hug!"

He grinned, set his bags down, and pulled his father into an embrace. "It's great to see you, Pop! It really is." He slapped his back a few times then released him. He looked past his shoulder and found Sabrina smiling in the front door entrance. "Hey... Mom?"

"Hell no, don't call me Mom! I'm too damn young for that shit!" She laughed and walked out toward him. "Get over here and let me squeeze your neck."

Her slender arms pulled Robert down to her level. He grinned and looked up at his father. "Good to see you, too."

"Woman, you're a year younger than I am. You're old enough to..."

She immediately let Robert go and turned on her fiancé. "You say it; the couch is yours, even on our damn wedding night! Got it?"

He chuckled. "Yes, dear."

"Good boy." She smiled and Makayla laughed. "Thank you, honey, for picking him up."

"Oh, it wasn't a problem at all, Aunt Sabrina. We had a good ride and some time to talk. Although, he did tear up my sign."

"I did? Oh yeah, I did. What the hell was that?"

"That was an idea between me, Aunt Sabrina, and my bestie, Lexi."

Robert furrowed his brows, not recognizing the name. "Who's Lexi? Is that someone I know? If some strange chick is making signs about me, I'd like to at least know who I'm dealing with." He crossed his strong arms over his broad chest.

Makayla just shrugged. "Guess you'll figure that out at the bonfire later."

CHAPTER 2

*A*fter getting settled in, Robert took a shower and shaved. He dried his body off then wiped his hand across the mirror. He sighed and looked at his reflection. "Bonfire, beer, and women." He smirked. "Damn, it's good to be back."

He pulled on a light blue polo which made his own baby blues pop. A pair of Cinch jeans followed that before he pulled on an old pair of cowboy boots he'd bought a few years back. Georgia was no Texas but seeing a cowboy here and there wasn't uncommon.

"Come on, don't you have a lasso and whip or something?" He recalled the words of his ex-girlfriend who had tried to dress the part of a rodeo princess, but failed to meet everyone's expectations. She looked more like a wanna-be princess who rode in a motor pool, waving at her wanting fans. He shook off the memory as he fed a leather belt through his belt loops.

"I thought you might be able to use this." Sabrina's voice came in behind him. He turned and found her holding a straw cowboy hat. "Your father never wears it; it's pretty much brand new."

"Thank you." He took it and slipped it onto his head, the fit perfect.

"Oh honey, those girls will fall over themselves to get to you tonight. Wow!" She smiled, turned, and left the room.

He chuckled, then turned back to the mirror and looked. Memories of Texas and of rodeos, stock shows, and riding the trails came flooding back. Damn, he had missed this shit.

"Well, don't you look all stylish in your crisp jeans and a cowboy hat?"

He grinned and looked at Makayla in the mirror. "I don't exactly have Wranglers you know."

"How's that Garth Brooks song go? *'Blame it all on my roots, I showed up in boots, and ruined your black tie affair?'*"

"'*The last one you thought you'd see there?*'" He grinned and she nodded.

"Exactly. You ready? Because the party has started and you're the main attraction!"

"What the hell did you do?" The look of fear stuck his face for a moment.

"Who me? Nothing." The over-enunciation was clear.

He shook his head. "You'll pay for this if you get me in trouble or in the paper."

"Don't worry. It's just a few friends coming together for a party. Nothing more," she smiled.

"Uh huh. Let's go, Trouble." He led her out by the small of her back, grinning at what was yet to come. "By the way, you look real nice in that top. Brings out your eyes." She smiled at him.

"Thanks, cuz." He ran his hands down his shirt, feeling a bit pre-occupied.

"You're welcome. And I'll take you shopping for something more… appropriate."

"You dissing my style?" He grinned.

"Not at all! Now, let's go."

They headed out toward the lake after the sun had set. She pulled into a spot between a few other trucks, a few cars, and a motorcycle. "So, how many people did you invite exactly?" He asked her.

"Oh, just a few friends, who have friends, who have friends. You know how it is." She waved him off and got out of the truck. Meeting him around the front of it, she said, "And if you're lucky, someone will be muddin' tonight."

"Is that someone you?"

"Oh hell no! I don't take my Sassy Thing in the mud unless it's raining."

"Or if I tease her about being a girly girl." A voice came around and Makayla squealed and jumped.

"Don't grab my ass like that, Conner! Damn you, you scared me! And for your information, I'm NOT a girly girl!" She followed him and smacked his arm.

He chuckled and pulled her in for a hug, then kissed her.

"Whoa, who're you?" Robert asked.

"That depends, who're you?" Conner responded pulling Makayla closer as if he were staking claim on her.

"Conner, this is my cousin, Bobby Ray. Bobby Ray, this is my man candy, Conner."

"Man candy?" Conner and Robert asked at the same time. Conner chuckled and looked back at Robert. "Any cousin, friend, or whatever is a friend of mine. Conner Whitmore. How are ya?" Conner held his hand out.

Robert shook it with a smile. "Robert, nice to meet you."

Makayla rolled her eyes. "Trust me, it's Bobby Ray."

"Bobby Ray Shaw in the FLESH!" Another voice called from behind them and Robert turned.

"Damn son! Brad is that you? Been a long ass time!" Robert clapped his hand against Brad's then pulled him into a hug.

"Sure as hell has! What the hell took you so long to get back here?" His friend pulled back and smiled.

"Hell man, I've been damn busy, you know?"

"Yeah, I know; it's cool," Brad said.

13

A little ways in the distance, a female's voice yelled before she screamed. "FUCK YOU!" She stormed back toward the bonfire and walked past Robert, brushing against his shoulder.

"Excuse me," he offered.

She turned to give whoever she bumped a piece of her mind and when her eyes caught his, she stopped. For a moment, it seemed as if his eyes mesmerized hers. "Pardon me," she whispered. "I didn't see you."

"It's no problem." He tipped his hat to her and offered a smile. Her long blond hair was a little windblown, her skin looked sun kissed and her lips were beautiful... damn if he didn't know better, he would lean in and kiss her right then. "Anything I can help you with? I couldn't help overhear you yelling."

"Yeah girl, we all heard you." Makayla asked. "Blaine?"

She blinked, looking at Robert. He smiled a little more, thinking he had no chance if this Blaine was in the picture. *No man in his right mind would let this fine, young thing wander off. Damn, she's gorgeous.*

"Huh?" She snapped herself out of it then turned around. "Yeah, we're through. I'm so over his shit. I called it off and he tried to defend being with other women, as if there is any excuse for his actions." She crossed her arms over her chest and shook her head. "Should have known this stardom would go to his head. Where's the booze? I need something to drink!"

The beautiful stranger walked away and Robert stepped closer to his cousin. "Who the hell is that? Damn, she's beautiful." He grinned watching her tight ass against her short shorts. Her legs were slender, but strong... athletic. He thought of them wrapped around his waist and he rubbed at his crotch.

"Nice. Down boy." Makayla rolled her eyes. "Do you not recognize her?"

He shook his head. "Not in the least."

"Dude," Brad walked up and clapped his shoulder. "That there is Lexi Griffin."

"Lexi Griffin? As in Alexis Griffin?" Robert couldn't take his eyes off her.

"The one in the same," Brad offered.

"Damn, I remember her skinny as a rail, braces, and pig tails." Robert wiped his hand down his face. "Fuck me, she grew up."

"Hell yeah, she did," Brad offered.

"She's also my best friend, the one who helped make your sign." Makayla stated.

"Really? You gonna hook me up?" As his cousin was about to answer, he shook his head, and held up a hand. "Nah, I got this," he smirked.

"Yeah, good luck with that," Makayla grinned. "Try to top being a rock star. Blaine dated her for a few years before he was signed. He's barely home and the fucker cheated on her even before he was making it big. She was too naïve to see it... or didn't want to see it."

"Yeah, he cheated a lot," responded Conner.

"Damn. Well, that explains the outburst." Robert watched her across the bonfire then shook his head. "Well, I'm here for the summer and I have no problem being the rebound guy to get her over it."

Brad laughed, and then led him over to the cooler. "Watch out, she's a tough one." He lifted the lid and pulled out two bottle necks. "Coors Light?"

"Tough, huh?" Robert took the beer. "You really stereotype southerners, you know that?"

Conner chuckled and followed up behind them. "You can take the guy outta the country but you can't take the country out of the guy." He shrugged. "It's what we do. Kick shit and drink beer."

They laughed and opened the bottles. "Damn, it's good to be home." Robert kept his eyes on Lexi and occasionally, caught her looking over at him. He thought he saw her smile.

~

"*M*akayla, is that your cousin? Bobby Ray? The good lord definitely blessed that man with the body of a god!" She grinned at Robert then quickly averted her gaze.

"So are you over Blaine, then? Bobby Ray is only here for the summer. Don't get involved with him. You'll regret it."

"What? Number one, why would I get involved with him and number two, why would I regret it?" She shifted her weight onto her right foot, letting her weight settle on her hip. She crossed her arms over her chest, pushing her breasts up in her halter.

"Did you not hear me say he's only here for the summer? If you get involved with him, you'll only hurt yourself that much more. Bobby Ray isn't a player, Lexi. Not in the sense of love'em and leave'em. He's got a lot to offer a girl and honestly, he needs someone who will treat him right."

"Well, you're making me sound like some kind of whore," Lexi responded. She rolled her eyes and shifted her feet underneath her.

Makayla shook her head. "I'm not trying to, just trying to warn you and keep you from making another mistake. I hate to see you hurting like this over Blaine. He did you bad, girl. Real bad. Oh and the second part? His stepdad is a Senator from Georgia. Anything he does out of line could get him, and his family, in trouble."

"And you think I'm that kinda trouble?" Lexi wasn't sure if she wanted to laugh or slap her best friend.

"Well, no I don't. But I know Blaine is and if he decides to come back into town and Bobby Ray in the picture? Yeah that could get nasty real quick."

"Speaking of getting nasty," Conner wrapped an arm around her shoulders and kissed her temple. "How about we go muddin'?"

"How about cliff diving instead?" Lexi offered. She looked over when Robert walked up and she felt her face pink with blush. "I mean, if y'all aren't too scared of the dark."

Robert grinned. "I might be scared. Would you hold my hand?" He took a pull from his beer.

"Only if you're nice when I hold it. If you're lucky, I might jerk it for you." She winked and turned on her heel, walking away from them. The sway in her ass didn't go unnoticed.

"Good God, I'm in trouble." Robert chuckled and shook his head.

~

*R*obert stood toward the edge of the cliff and looked down. He raised his brows and asked, "So how deep is the water down there?"

"Deep enough, I suppose," Lexi answered him when she joined him at his side. She looked over the edge as the wind blew. Her hair tumbled over her shoulder and tickled against Robert's arm. He inhaled and her perfume invaded his senses. "Why," she looked up at him, "you scared?"

He grinned and locked eyes with her. "With you by my side, what could I possibly be scared of?"

Lexi held her breath for a second and her smile almost faltered. She blinked and felt her mouth go dry. "I'll, umm..." She turned and walked into the woods.

Makayla looked between him and Lexi, then back to him. "What the hell did you say?"

"Nothing. She asked if I was scared and I told her not if she was by my side." She slapped his arm so hard, it echoed. A few ooh's were heard around them when Robert flinched. "What the HELL woman?"

"What the hell 'me'? What the hell 'you'! You don't tell a girl you just met she'll be by your side! Especially when..." Makayla stopped talking when she heard Lexi scream... except it wasn't a scream of fear; it was a scream of joy.

Lexi came barreling out of the woods in her bra and panties.

She ran toward the cliff's edge and glanced at Robert. "DON'T BE A PUSSY!" She laughed and lunged off the edge, aiming straight down toward the water.

"HOLY SHIT!" Robert yelled and watched her as she landed in the water with a splash. He watched for a moment then breathed a sigh of relief when she came up for air.

Then he laughed when he heard her voice echo up from the depths of the water, "PUSSY!"

"I'll show her pussy." He took off his polo and tossed it to the ground.

"Dude, that didn't sound right, but I got your back on this one. No, Makayla, let him." Conner held his hands up to her. "She wants to have fun and he wants some action. Let them play. Now c'mon!" He took her hand and pulled her away, but not before she said her piece.

"Bobby Ray! Tread lightly!" She smiled and tangled her body around Conner's.

"Thanks, cuz!" Robert laughed as he pulled off his boots. He unbuttoned his jeans and pushed them down, standing naked save for his boxers. "Y'all don't bother coming down unless you hear us yell snake." He chuckled, then ran toward the edge and jumped. He yelled on the way down and, as soon as he hit the water, Lexi's voice sang up in laughter.

Makayla smiled at hearing her best friend laugh, something she hadn't heard in a long time.

CHAPTER 3

*R*obert came up for air and shook the water from his face. "Lexi, never call a man a pussy."

She smiled while treading water. "Well, you looked like you needed a reason to jump."

He moved closer to her and looked her over. Her hair was smoothed completely back over her head, wet. Her blue eyes reflected the moonlight and her skin... damn, her skin was perfection. He wanted to pull her close and wrap his arms around her. He wanted to kiss her, have his hands on her body. She was downright sexy as hell.

Suddenly, he flinched when water was splashed on his face. "Stop looking at me like I'm a damn meal, Bobby Ray." She smiled then laid her back on the water. She kicked at the water, putting a little distance between them.

He watched her as her breasts crested over the top of the water. He felt himself drool a little... or maybe it was the water running down from his scalp. He grinned, and then decided to have a little fun with his new friend.

Robert held his breath, went under water, and swam toward her. He looked up and found her floating. He reached up and touched the back of her leg. He heard her scream and she flailed against the water. He swam closer, hoping not to get kicked and he wrapped his arms around her waist, pulling her back to his chest. "Hey now, I got you, don't worry. I won't let you drown," he whispered in her ear.

Lexi allowed him to hold her as she enjoyed the feeling of his chest against her back. She closed her eyes for a moment and allowed herself to feel him fully. When Blaine's image popped into her mind, she decided enough was enough.

"Bobby Ray, as much as I appreciate your efforts in an attempt to drown me, just to save my life..." She pulled herself from his arms then turned toward him. She tried not to make it obvious she was staring. This close to him, she was able to get a really good look at him... and his well-chiseled chest. "Damn."

"Excuse me?" He asked then grinned.

"What? Oh hell!" She blushed and turned away from him. "I didn't mean to say that! Oh my god, I'm so embarrassed!"

"Okay, well, you're damn hot, Lexi. So... we're even." He moved toward her and turned her around to face him. "Nah girl, it's okay. Don't be embarrassed. I kinda like having an effect on you." He winked.

"Well, I would rather you didn't," she averted her gaze. "I'm, well, I guess I'm in transition."

He furrowed his brows. "Transition? I'm not sure I follow."

She looked up at him, opened her mouth to say something, and then closed it. "You know what? Doesn't matter." She smiled then turned to swim toward shore.

"Where you going?" He started to follow and noticed she was trying to pull ahead, put distance between them. "Lexi look, I'm sorry if..."

She cut him off and turned around. "Bobby Ray, I don't know what you're after here with me, but my boyfriend of almost three years... well he broke my heart. I'm not ready to jump into the fire quite yet, you know? And you're only here for the summer, right?

So I don't see where this," she motioned between them, "could even go anywhere."

"I'm not looking to get into anything, either. But listen to me when I tell you this," he gave her an honest look and held his ground as he moved toward her. "I came back here for my father's wedding. I had no idea about this party, about you, or what happened between the two of you. Quite frankly, I'm not sorry it happened." She opened her mouth to protest and he held up his hands. "Let me finish. What I'm trying to say is that you're better off not being lied to and treated like you don't mean anything. That son of a bitch has no idea how beautiful you are. Damn, it's his loss, Lexi. If he can't see that, then he's a damned fool." He shook his head and swam past her, feeling this was the end of anything ever getting started with her.

Well, that was until he felt her grab his leg. "Wait, Bobby Ray." Her hand ran down to his ankle and she tugged lightly then reached for his arm.

He stopped and turned to look at her. "Yeah?" He could see the vulnerability on her face, the longing for something, the need for his arms around her.

She moved closer toward him in the water, and looked up into his eyes. "You really mean all that?"

He nodded. "We may have known each other since we were kids, but hell Lexi, tonight is like meeting you again for the first time."

"Please, don't lie to me. I've been lied to so much."

"Why would I lie to you? We've not seen each other since, what; we were ten, eleven years old? I have nothing to hide here. If he's ass enough to walk away from you then it's his loss."

"I can't believe I'm about to do this."

"Do what?" he asked her just as she jumped into his arms and pressed her lips to his.

He grunted, catching her then wasting no time putting his arms around her, pulling her close. He deepened the kiss and her arms moved up around his neck. Her breasts pressed against his chest and she whimpered softly against his lips.

"Lexi," he whispered her name against her lips.

She pulled away and rested her forehead against his. When she opened her eyes and looked at him, she smiled. "I think we need to get out of here. If your hard on is any indication, we need to stop."

He chuckled and reached down between them, adjusting himself in his loose boxers. "You excite me. That's a very good thing."

She smiled then pulled out of his arms. "I work at the tack store in town. I work tomorrow. Come by and see me, preferably with clothes on." She grinned wider. "I would rather with clothes off, but if we are to talk, clothes on is a must."

He chuckled and nodded. "Clothing is overrated. Tack store tomorrow. I'll come by and get you for lunch. Sound good?"

"Sure does, cowboy." She smiled and swam toward the shore.

"I'm as far from a cowboy as they get," he mumbled with a grin on his lips. "This summer just got much more interesting." He chuckled again then began swimming toward the shore.

Lexi climbed out of the water and Robert watched her slender frame climb up the hill. His smile continued to grow, especially when she glanced at him over her shoulder. She smiled then ran up the hill to gather her clothes. Robert groaned and fell back into the water, feeling a set of blue balls staking their claim.

$\sim$

"*Makayla!*" Lexi called her best friend while wringing out her hair. "Bitch, you didn't tell me Bobby Ray got damn hot!"

"What the hell! He's my COUSIN!" Makayla shook her head with a laugh. "It's nice to see you smile again."

Lexi grinned as she pulled on her shorts and halter-top. She pulled her hair up into a tie then rested her hands on her hips. "It feels good to smile for a reason, rather than faking it."

Just then, her phone chimed. Lexi looked at the screen and found "Blaine, my love" across the screen. She rolled her eyes and tossed her phone into her purse.

"You're not even going to read it?" Makayla asked.

"Why do I need to? He's just going to give me another bullshit excuse as to who the flavor of the week is and why he fell into weakness. Having a rock star as a boyfriend is a damn joke." She continued to vent as Robert made his way up the bank. "All the bitches throwing their panties at him. I can't put myself in his place but if I were a dude, I guess I'd find it hard to say no when every single hoochie is throwing their shit in his face."

Robert listened in on their conversation while he pulled on his clothes. Leaning against the tree next to him, Brad took a pull on his beer then motioned to the women. "Any man would be lucky to have her on their arm."

"She kissed me." Robert grinned then pulled his polo on over his head.

"Dude, do what?" Conner chuckled then slapped his shoulder. "Welcome home, Bobby Ray."

"Seriously man, call me Robert."

"BOBBY RAY!" Makayla shouted. Lexi looked over her shoulder at him then giggled.

"Dammit," Robert sighed. "I'll never live that shit down."

"Why would you? It's cute," Lexi told him. Robert gave her a sideways grin.

Conner looked between the two of them then shook his head. "Alright woman, let's get you home. Where are your keys?"

"No way, Conner! My baby, I'm driving." She waved her keys in front of him then snatched them into her palm, teasing him.

"Oh, you're in for it now!" Conner laughed as he took off after his girlfriend. She giggled and ran toward her truck.

"Well hell, how am I getting home?" Robert asked.

"Umm," Lexi began then shuffled her feet slightly. "I can take you, I suppose." Her voice had softened and her gaze slowly lifted up to his.

Robert found himself staring at her, at a loss for words. A hand gripped his shoulder as the words, "tell her yes," were whispered.

Brad patted his shoulder with a smile, and climbed into his own truck, headed home.

"Yes, thank you." Robert walked toward her then looked around as the sounds of the party begin to die down. "Is that okay?"

"Sure, as long as you don't try anything." She smiled then turned, walking toward her car.

"What would constitute anything?" He grinned, followed her, and they climbed into her car.

CHAPTER 4

$\mathcal{L}$exi pulled up to Robert's home and placed her car into park. She reached up and pushed her blond hair behind her ear, then looked over to him. "Thanks for a fun evening tonight. I surely wasn't expecting it and definitely didn't expect... you."

He grinned then reached for her hand. He pulled it to his lips and kissed it. "Well, I'm happy to have obliged."

"You know where the tack store is in town?" She asked as she intertwined her fingers with his. Robert's hands were big, but not huge. They were soft, but also callused. She had a brief image of his hands on her body and she felt her face blush. She was thankful for the darkness of her car. Twenty-two years old and still blushing around men. She wanted to laugh at herself but instead, pursed her lips.

"I have no idea where it is." He chuckled and shrugged. "But since my Pop lives on a farm I'm positive he or Sabrina has an idea." He leaned in and kissed her softly on her cheek, then whispered, "Thank you for the ride home."

She turned her face slightly toward his and their lips were just slightly apart from one another. "You're welcome," she breathed.

Robert looked from her eyes to her lips and back again. He leaned into her and their noses brushed together slightly. Lexi closed her eyes and her lips parted. He swallowed then slowly pulled away.

When she felt the absence, she opened her eyes just as the dome light came on. She offered a smile. "I'll see you tomorrow, then."

"You can count on it." He stepped out of her car and shut the door. He walked around the hood toward the house.

Her eyes watched him and the tight jeans holding his ass. She couldn't help the smile on her lips. She shook her head and smiled, putting her car into drive. Suddenly, she jumped at a tap on her window.

Robert was there, bent over, with an urgent look on his face. She quickly pressed the down button for the window. "What happened?" She asked. He quickly dipped in, cupped her face, and kissed her.

He pulled away then looked at her with a smile. "It would have been a damn shame to let you leave with a kiss good night."

She blushed and this time, she didn't care if he saw it or not. "Good night, Bobby Ray." She smiled again and, as the window rolled up, she took off down the road.

~

*T*he next morning Robert woke up with a smile on his face. He stretched and groaned, then sat up to the smell of bacon and eggs. He rubbed the sleep from his eyes then stood, making his way toward the bathroom for a shower and shave.

"How was your night?" Sabrina's voice sounded in his bedroom as she peeked in.

"I'm dressed, it's okay, come on in." Robert yawned and stretched again. "I had a great night, thanks for asking." He smiled.

"So I've heard." She leaned against the wall and her smirk didn't go unnoticed.

"What?" He asked her.

"Makayla called this morning, wanted to know if Lexi dropped you off or not."

"Oh," Robert smiled at the thought of Lexi, and Sabrina laughed. "What's funny?"

"Oh nothing, just summer love." She grinned then left the room. "Breakfast is ready when you come down."

"Alright, thank you." He walked toward the bathroom and turned on the shower. After brushing his teeth, he stepped under the shower head and closed his eyes at the hot water running down his body.

Lexi Griffin was all grown up and damn if she wasn't sexy as hell. She kissed him and she's single now. "Well, sort of," he told himself. *Tread lightly*; Makayla's words come back to him. "Hell, I'm not going to be her boyfriend or anything. I'm leaving soon, anyway," he told himself.

After turning off the shower, he towel dried his body, and wrapped the towel around his waist. He opened his suitcase and found it empty. "What the..." He made his way to the dresser in the room and found his clothes tucked neatly in place. "Well hell, that was kind of her." He walked to the closet and found his clothes hung nicely.

He thought of Makayla's offer to take him shopping. There were probably a few rodeos in town, but mainly, he missed riding. He wanted to saddle up a horse, go out on the trail, and if time allowed in her schedule, take Lexi with him.

He pulled on a fitted t-shirt and his Cinch jeans, boots, and a belt. He made his way downstairs and found his father reading the morning news. "Morning, Pop."

The paper was lowered and he grinned. "Hey son. Hungry?"

"Yeah, smells great. Sabrina, thanks for unpacking for me. I trust you didn't find my porn?"

"Sure did and confiscated it. Your father and I watched it last night."

James blinked at her then looked at Robert. "You seriously brought porn with you?" He busted out a belly laugh.

"Hell no, I didn't bring no damn porn! I wasn't expecting her to call me out like that!" Robert chuckled then looked to Sabrina. "Yeah, you fit right in with us."

"Thank you," she bowed playfully then pointed toward the kitchen. "Eat up as much as you want. If you're still hungry, well there's a store down the road." She grinned and he chuckled.

"Nah, this'll be enough. Thank you."

"You're welcome, Sugar." She kissed his cheek then took her seat next to James.

"Pop, can you tell me where the tack store is in town?" He filled his plate with food then took a seat at the table. He took a bite of the eggs and nodded. "Damn, these are good."

"Thank you," she told him.

"You bet." His father went through the directions on how to find the store while Robert ate and nodded a few times.

"Easy 'nuff. Thanks, Pop." He finished up then rinsed off his plate in the sink. "Can I borrow a car or truck for today? I can get a rental today so I don't inconvenience anyone."

"Not a problem, son. Just let us know when you're ready to go to town for the rental. We'll drive you."

"Appreciate that."

Robert headed outside toward the stalls where the horses were kept. He brought out a black leather saddle from the tack room and a dark blue saddle pad. Grabbing reins and the bit, he walked toward the door that was labeled "Dixie."

"Well, hello there beautiful," he started. The mare nodded her head a few times then leaned over the door to smell his hand. Robert uncurled his fingers to a few treats, which she quickly devoured.

He led Dixie out of her stall and hooked her up to the leads in the walkway. After brushing her down and picking out her hoofs, he saddled her up and readied her bridle.

Pushing on his sunglasses, he led Dixie out of the barn then climbed onto her saddle. He pushed the straw hat Sabrina loaned him the other night on his head.

"Be good to me, girl. It's been a while," Robert grinned to himself. He gently nudged the mare in her sides and she began to walk at a leisurely pace. The pair entered the woods on the trail and took in the best of Mother Nature.

Birds sang in the trees and the breeze blew gently in the air. Lexi came to mind and he grinned as he thought about the kiss they shared.

"She would love it out here," he told himself. Dixie leaned over and pulled a few leaves off a nearby tree. "This isn't an all you can eat buffet, my dear." He chuckled and patted the mare's neck.

Robert lost track of time, enjoying the sounds of nature around him, he decided to head back toward home. The sun was warm and he began to sweat; so did Dixie.

He took her back into the barn and hooked her up in the hallway again. After removing her saddle, pad, and bridle, he decided a good hose down would do the mare some good. He came back with the water hose and turned it on. He sprayed her down then allowed Dixie to drink from the hose. Of course, putting the hose to her mouth wasn't the best idea. She got more of the water on him than what went into her mouth.

After running the water comb over her body, Robert put Dixie back in her stall. He patted her neck, "Thanks for the ride today, girl. I'll be seeing you soon."

Dixie made a few sounds as Robert left her stall. He put away his supplies then grabbed a few handfuls of her treats. He laid them in her feeding bucket and she immediately went after them.

Making his way back toward the house, Sabrina laughed as Robert entered the house.

"So did any of the water actually get where it was intended? Or just on you?"

"Cute. I'm headed up for a shower then I'll be taking off. I just rode Dixie. She's great."

"Yeah, she's my girl. Maybe next time we go to the auction, we can pick one out for you." She smiled at Robert.

"Wow, my very own pony?" He chuckled, teasing her. Nothing in his words was harsh and she stuck her tongue out at him.

"Go shower; you smell," she grinned and walked out of the room. He chuckled and ascended the stairs to his room.

After his shower, Robert dressed and made his way down to the kitchen, finding the keys to the Ford Dually on the table. He collected them then hustled out to the driveway and opened up the truck. He smiled at the fresh interior, enjoying the new car smell, and climbed inside. The truck roared to life and he put it into gear and headed toward town... toward Lexi.

~

*B*ack in the tack room, Lexi picked up and shifted bags of feed. She wiped the sweat from her forehead and smiled. She found herself counting down the time until she could take her lunch break and see Bobby Ray.

"LEXI GRIFFIN!"

Lexi shot up and turned around, startled, when a voice yelled her name. She saw her other best friend, Abby Masters. The girl was beautiful, tall, and lean with long blonde hair. Her eyes were as brown as dark chocolate and her skin tan, almost olive. Abby had modeled a few times and considered making a career out of it. Her senior year in high school she suddenly decided against it. Some said she didn't make it; others said she was kicked out for trying to sex up the manager. Lexi never judged her and never asked any questions.

Lexi grinned and wiped her hands on her jeans. "Hey, girl!"

"When the hell were you going to tell me Bobby Ray Shaw was back in town?"

"Well, I just found out myself last night, Abby. Matter of fact," she glanced to the clock again, "he's coming by to pick me up for lunch. You want to stay and say hi?" She smiled at her friend.

"Of course!" She drew out her southern twang and leaned against the wall. "I heard he got all kinds of hot and has more money than God!"

"Well yeah, he got hot!" Lexi felt her face blush and she lowered her gaze. "But really Abby? More money than God?" She looked up and found her friend watching her. "What?"

"Blaine?" Abby raised her brows.

"Yeah, what about him? We broke up." She turned around and grabbed another feed bag and tossed it.

"Ohmigawd!" She exclaimed all in one word. "When were you gonna tell me?"

"There's not much to tell. He's a pig and I'm through being used. I'm worth more than that."

"But he's BLAINE! He's a rock star!"

"Then you date him," she said a little callously. "Look Abby, he broke my heart. I'm done. I want to move on and honestly, I don't have to explain my reasons why. No offense, but I just don't want to talk about it."

"Hey," she held her hands up. "I'm sorry, I didn't mean to tread."

Lexi smiled. "It's okay, you didn't." Her eyes darted past her and a smile formed on her lips.

Abby watched as her tanned face began to turn a shade of pink. She turned and looked behind her and found a very handsome man not too far behind her. "Well, if it isn't Bobby Ray Shaw, in the flesh!" She walked over to him and opened her arms in a hug. "C'mere and give me some love! Damn, it's been a long time!"

Robert looked from Lexi to Abby and smiled. "Aww, Abby. Yes, I remember you. How are you girl?" He hugged her and felt her press herself against him a little too closely. He cleared his throat and looked at Lexi. She pursed her lips not to laugh. *Oh, she'll pay for that later,* he told himself.

After he pulled himself free from the Abby's grip, he side stepped her and walked toward Lexi. He grinned and reached for a loose strand of her hair, moving it from her face. "Hey."

"Hey yourself," she replied. *Oh damn, he smells good,* she told herself. She looked over at Abby with a grin and found a disgusted look on her face instead. Lexi's smile faltered. "Abby, are you okay?"

"What?" Abby smiled and nodded. "Oh yes, perfect. Well, if you two will excuse me, I have somewhere to be." She smiled and ducked out, leaving them alone.

"What's her deal?" Robert asked.

"Okay, I love that girl to pieces. She and Makayla have been there for me through this whole... Blaine crap." She motioned with her hands and Robert nodded. "But she gets upset if the attention from a... well a hot guy," she felt her face blush again, and this time, the night skies couldn't disguise it, "isn't all over her."

"Ahh, so you think I'm a hot guy?" He asked as he stepped closer toward her.

She fanned her face. "Is it hot in here?"

He grinned. "Not really, but I'll pretend if it helps."

She looked up and seeing him smile, she grinned, and then shook her head. "What am I going to do with you?"

He shrugged then lightly touched her hand. "I'm hoping to find out."

She blushed again, and looked down. "Let me go clock out and we can go. Okay?" She looked back up and he nodded. "Just wait for me out front. I'll meet you out there."

"Alright." He grinned at her again, then turned and walked out the way he came.

She watched his ass the entire time he walked away from her.

She shook her head, smiling before she turned to clock out and wash up. "Damn, that boy has an ass."

Robert leaned against the register counter and looked around the store. Saddles for English and Western style riding, harnesses, reins, saddle blankets and every type of feed, bot remover, and bucket you could think of for livestock were set up on the shelves and throughout the store.

"Alright, you ready?" Lexi walked toward the counter with a purse over her shoulder and she pushed a pair of shades onto her face. "I'm starving."

He nodded with a smile. "Yeah, let's go." He appreciated a woman who would eat in front of him. He laid his hand on the small of her back and escorted her toward the front door. "Where's a good place to go for lunch around here?"

"Well, we can hit up Italian food, Chinese, or Mexican. Oh, and I don't mean Taco Bell." She grinned and looked over at him.

He grinned. "I'd hope not." He opened the truck door for her and watched her as she climbed inside. "It's been a long while since I've had real Mexican food; sounds good to me." He closed her door, walked around the front of the truck, and climbed inside. Starting it up, he glanced over at her and found her fiddling with her fingers. "Lexi, if you're not ready for a date…"

She immediately looked up and shook her head. "No, no it's not that. It's just…" She looked down again then shrugged. "This is… it's just so new for me." She looked back at him again with a soft smile. "Just be patient with me, please?"

He nodded and put the truck into gear. He turned and grabbed onto her seat as he backed out of the store parking lot. "No pressure. We're just friends, getting reacquainted." He winked at her then put it into drive, taking off down the road.

"Friends who are getting reacquainted who also kiss? Doesn't sound normal to me." She laughed then visibly relaxed in the seat.

"Well, if said friend is hot, hell yeah, I'm gonna do my best to kiss her." He chuckled then turned the radio volume down. "Lexi,

I'm serious, okay? No pressure. You're just getting out of your relationship and I'm just here for the summer."

She nodded. "I understand." She looked out the window for a moment and couldn't help but think how Bobby Ray has been more of a gentleman in the single day she'd spent with him than Blaine had been in over three years. "I still want to have fun with you, if that's allowed?" She looked over at him shyly with a grin on her lips.

He blinked and felt his mouth go dry. He looked back toward the road and nodded, then grinned. "You bet your fine ass it's allowed."

She smiled and crossed her legs in the seat as they drove into town.

~

*T*he waiter took the menus from them and left them to their silence. Lexi looked around the restaurant and Robert, for the first time in a long while, felt at a loss for words.

At the University, he was up for debate at any given time; it's what he did. He planned to go into family law. He wanted to protect those who couldn't protect themselves. Too many times he'd read stories of families losing everything because their sole breadwinner passed away.

"What's on your mind?" Lexi asked him.

"Hmm?" He glanced up and smiled. Her blue eyes captivated him. She'd laid her hands on the table and he wanted to reach over and take one. "School, my studies, debate," he shrugged.

"Oh, are you on the debate team?" She raised her brows. "You don't really strike me as the type."

"What's that supposed to mean?" He asked.

"Oh, I didn't mean anything by that. You seem to be more... oh I don't know, the jock I guess? Like into college football, maybe play for your university. Stuff like that."

"Well Lexi, there's a lot about me you don't know. Hell, there's a lot about you I don't know," he said. "I guess spending time with each other will catch us up on everything we've missed." The waiter brought over two sweet teas and laid down straws. After thanking him, Robert continued. "I look forward to learning about you, too. That is, if you decide to tell me all about Lexi Griffin."

She smiled. "There's not much to tell, really." She opened her straw, put it into her tea, and took a sip. "Wow, that's sweet." She smacked her lips twice and Robert smiled. "My life has really been wrapped up around Blaine and his rise to stardom. I haven't really done much for myself; outside of working at the tack store I'm afraid." She lowered her gaze to her fingers while she fiddled with her napkin.

Robert watched her for a moment and tried to imagine her world for a moment. He thought of her following this Blaine around, thought of her hanging onto his every word, then thought of him walking all over her like she was a damn doormat. "Right. Well, then it's my personal honor to allow you to discover yourself and what you like. I'd be honored to help in your journey of enlightenment. Who knows, maybe you'll pick up a new skill."

She looked up with a smile, appreciating his words. She ran her hand through her hair then tucked it behind her ear. "What kind of new skill?"

"Hmm... I'm thinking... needlework."

"What?" She furrowed her brows, completely caught off guard by his answer. He laughed and she shook her head. "Real funny. I'll have you know I can sew without a machine. Thank you very much!" She took another sip of her tea.

"I have no doubt you have great skills with a needle. In all seriousness, I plan on taking you outside your comfort zone as much as I can while I'm here." He sipped his tea and she grinned. "Wow, yeah that is sweet. Whoa, not quite what I get in Georgia." He took another sip then shuddered slightly. "Damn. Anyway, back to what I was saying. I plan on horseback trail riding, camping, taking in a rodeo or two, maybe even a few movies. Oh and I'm the best man in a wedding and, if you would, I'd like you to be my date," he winked.

"All of that sounds intriguing, but most of it I've done before." She shrugged, teasing him. "Well, except for your father's wedding, that'll be a first." He pointed to her and winked. "There are a few things I'd like to try, if you're game."

"Name it. What'cha got?"

"Rock climbing and jet skiing. I've not done either and I'd love to try!" She grinned, bouncing a little in her excitement.

He nodded and pulled out his phone to check the time just as the waiter came with their food. "Aww, here we go. Damn, it's been a while since I've had real enchiladas. And before you even suggest it, Taco Bell doesn't count."

She laughed and opened her napkin, before she placed it on her lap. "I never would."

They enjoyed their lunch, and had casual conversation about his school and law. He told her about the debates he'd been a part of, the work he'd done with his stepdad in his political office and what Robert would like to do once he graduates college. "How about you? School plans?" He took a bite, savoring the flavor.

She dabbed her lips with her napkin then sat it down. "I was going to college here at UTA, studying large equine veterinary medicine. Some issues came up at home and I have had to take year off to help out my mom."

"Oh, okay. Have things settled so you can get back?" He asked, hoping he wasn't overstepping any boundaries.

She shook her head no. "A lot has happened since then. I would really like to go back," she gave him a sad smile, "but I don't think it's actually in the cards right now."

"Would it be okay to ask why? I don't want to overstep, so I hope this is okay."

She nodded and offered a smile. "It's fine, I don't mind." She sat back in her seat and thought for a moment, fiddling with her fingers again in her lap. "When Blaine took off last year, my time was really freed up. I went from having my life planned out twenty-four/seven, to twenty- four hours of nothing. It was quite an adjustment and my studies were all caught up. Then," she trailed off and adjusted herself in her seat. "About a year ago, there was an accident. My father..." She reached up and wiped a tear away.

"Lexi, it's okay you don't have to..."

"No, it's okay." She looked up and smiled, but it didn't reach her eyes. She sighed and continued. "My father had a heart attack one afternoon while he was on the tractor. He fell off."

"Oh my god, Lexi," he whispered.

She nodded. "It didn't run him over or anything, but when I saw the tractor sitting and not moving, well I knew something was wrong. I found him and called for my mama."

The waiter approached, asked if he could get them anything else. Robert looked up and shook his head. "Just the check, please." The waiter nodded and looked at Lexi then at Robert and gave him a scowl. *Oh perfect, he thinks I hurt her feelings.* Robert rolled his eyes.

Once the waiter left, she continued. "He didn't survive the heart attack. Mama was devastated. She went into a depression and most days, just sat and stared out the window. I tried talking to Blaine about it, but he was always too busy for me. I was hoping he would be able to help support our farm, you know, because he wanted to marry me. But I never could get him to say he would or wouldn't help.

"Then one day a woman answered his phone and called him baby. He told whoever she was to hang up and come back to bed, that his dick was hard again and she needed to suck it."

"What the fuck?" Robert asked.

She laughed a curt laugh then nodded. "Yeah, he did." She wiped her eyes with her napkin. "And trust me; these tears are not for him. I miss my daddy very much. Blaine can suck it for all I care."

Robert stood and she looked up at him, thinking they were about to leave. Then he walked over to her side of the booth and sat down. "Scoot over."

She moved over to give him room and watched him. "What are you..."

Without asking or hesitating, Robert pulled her into a hug and squeezed. "I'm so sorry you had to go through all of that. I'm so sorry, Lexi."

She sat there for a moment, stunned maybe. A stranger who came back into her life sat there hugging her, telling her he was sorry. She closed her eyes and leaned into him, taking comfort in his embrace. "Thank you," she whispered.

"If there's anything I can do," he told her.

She nodded against his chest. "Honestly, you're doing it." She pulled away and wiped her eyes again. "It's been a long time... well I'm not sure the last time I actually talked about this." She let out a huff mixed with a laugh.

"I have that effect on people." He grinned and pushed hair behind her ear. "You okay to leave and go for a walk?"

She nodded. "Yeah, that would be nice."

He stood and took her hand, helping her up. "What time do you get off tonight?"

"Seven." She put her purse on her shoulder.

"Alright. May I pick you up at your home, later? I'd like to take you home and make you dinner, if that's okay?"

She smiled and nodded.

"Good. I make a mean spaghetti. Actually," he grabbed the back of his neck. "That's about the extent of my culinary skills."

She smiled and this time, he noticed, it reached her eyes. "I love spaghetti."

He gave her a side grin. "Alright, let's get you back to work." He guided her out with a hand at her lower back.

He pulled into the store parking lot and put the truck into park. He cleared his throat and looked over at her.

"Thank you for lunch. This was nice," she told him.

"You're welcome." He reached for her hand and squeezed it. "I'll see you tonight, then?"

She nodded. She smiled then quickly leaned in and kissed his cheek. "Again, thank you for everything."

He smiled and watched her for a moment. His hand cupped her cheek as his fingers moved around her ear. "You're welcome." He leaned in to kiss her just as she pulled away. He groaned and let his head drop.

She smiled then giggled. "Till later, Bobby Ray."

He sighed and grinned at her. "Yes ma'am."

She shut the truck, walked back toward the tack store, and opened the door, not before she looked back with a smile.

He waved at her, then put the truck in reverse and backed out. Putting it into drive, he headed back toward home. He called his cousin on his blue tooth.

"Hey, Bobby Ray! What's up?" Makayla sounded like she was driving herself.

"I need a favor. Where's the clothing store around here."

Makayla squealed into the phone, and told him she'd meet him at his dad's house in half an hour.

CHAPTER 5

*B*laine swiped his finger across his phone and found a message from Lexi. He sighed and opened it. "Bitch probably asking for more money or for me to come home."

The woman of the moment by his side grinned. "You don't need that country girl. You got yourself a woman." She nibbled on his ear.

Blaine pushed her away and stared at his phone. "Pack your shit and get out."

"What?" She asked with shock in her eyes.

"You heard me." He turned away from her and walked into the other room. "You're a lousy fuck and can't suck dick to save your life. Get out or my guards will throw you out." He shut the bedroom door behind him then heard a glass shatter against it.

"FUCK YOU AND YOUR PENCIL DICK!" She grabbed her clothes, quickly got dressed, and headed out the door.

Normally Blaine didn't allow them to stay the night, but as drunk as he was there was no telling what he'd done. At least he still had his body parts and no new tattoos.

He opened Lexi's message and looked at it as fire set into his body.

Blaine, you're an asshole. I hope you get herpes. You don't deserve me. Fuck you and your band. We're over. Lexi.

"What the fuck?" He ran his hand through his shoulder length brown hair and found a message from Abby, Lexi's best friend.

Hey, good looking. There's a guy back in town and he's taking Lexi's attention away. I thought you should know. Let me know when you're in town, I'll come see you. XOXO Abby.

"Fuck this shit." He replied to Abby.

My tour will be close in Abilene. I have a three-day layover till we hit Austin. I'm coming back but don't tell her. I've got something in mind to surprise her with.

He pressed send then brought up Lexi's message again. "She better not be fucking anyone else."

Damn baby, why you gotta be so rough? Fuck me and my band? That's harsh, baby. And the only way I'll get herpes is from you. I'm using protection out here. What's your excuse?

He stared at his words for a moment and erased most of it before he hit send.

He tossed his phone on this bed and crossed the room to hit the shower and get ready for his afternoon before tonight's show. They would be leaving for Abilene soon and he needed to be ready for Lexi and whatever drama she'd gotten herself into.

*L*exi placed a pair of diamond earrings in her ears then slipped a necklace around her neck that had a teardrop diamond. It crested just above her bust line. "I don't want to give him a reason to stare." She smiled at herself then shrugged. "Hell, yeah, I do."

She turned and walked toward her closet to slip on her dress shoes. She'd not worn a dress in quite some time. Working in a tack store didn't exactly call for dresses, unless it was a sundress. It *was* hot outside. In addition, there was no lifting to be done.

The emerald green spaghetti strap dress was fitted around her bust. It flowed out from her waist to just above her knees. She closed her closet door then gave herself the once over. She sighed then smeared on lip gloss. "Well... this is what friends do, right?"

"Hardly." Lexi turned to the sound of her mother as she looked in on her daughter. "You look absolutely beautiful, honey."

She smiled. "Thank you, Mama." She walked over to her mother and hugged her.

"I wish your father were here to see you." She pulled back and looked at her daughter. "Blaine has no idea what he's missing. Good for nothing piece of shit that he is."

"Mama! Language!" Lexi smiled and for once, enjoyed trash talking her ex-boyfriend. "Actually no, go ahead. It feels good."

Her mother smiled then, as a knock sounded at the door, her brows shot up. "Oh, is that him? I bet it's him!"

"Mama, please don't embarrass me!" She followed her mother down the stairs, to the front door.

"Honey, go into the dining room. You need to make an entrance with that dress!"

Lexi rolled her eyes, then turned and walked toward the other room. She hated to be embarrassed by her mother, but then again, she'd not been this lively in quite a while. "It's nice seeing her having fun," she told herself.

Lexi's mother opened the door and she heard her exclaim,

"Well, you must be Bobby Ray Shaw! It's so nice to meet you! Please, do come in."

"Thank you, ma'am. Here, these are for you." Lexi heard what sounded like cellophane.

"Oh Bobby Ray, they are absolutely the most beautiful yellow roses I've ever seen in my life! Thank you!"

"Yellow roses?" Lexi whispered to herself. She peeked around the corner and found Bobby Ray watching her mother as she shuffled off toward the kitchen, probably looking for a vase. He was dressed in a button down white shirt that appeared to have been picked up from the cleaners, pressed jeans that had a nice shine to them and boots. Damn, that boy looked sexy as hell!

He folded his hands in front of him and began looking around the den. His eyes fell on pictures of Lexi as a child. As he stepped forward, she heard him chuckle.

She stepped out from behind her wall then leaned against it, studying him. "You had better be laughing because you think I'm cute, Bobby Ray." She smiled and watched as he turned to face her.

Robert's eyes widened as he took in the sight that was Lexi Griffin. His eyes went from hers to her dress, down her legs and to her shoes. He allowed his eyes to wander... slowly... back up her body again. As he stepped closer toward her, he noticed the diamond sitting just above her bust line. "Nice necklace."

She reached for it, fiddling with the charm. "You like that? I thought it was a nice added touch."

He swallowed and cleared his throat. "You look..." he shook his head then raised a hand, covering his mouth. He sighed and ran it down his face. "I have no words for how beautiful you look tonight."

"Aww, well isn't that the sweetest thing!" Lexi's mother came out of the kitchen with a big smile and her hands on her hips.

"Mama, please!" Lexi pleaded with her.

Robert chuckled. "Well, if you're ready? Your chariot awaits."

He motioned with his arm as if he were her stagecoach driver. She nodded then walked past him.

She kissed her mother on her cheek. "I'll be back later tonight, Mama. I love you."

"I love you, too, child. Take good care of my baby, Bobby Ray."

"Yes ma'am." He nodded toward her mother with a smile, and followed Lexi out the door, closing it behind him. "Your mom seems nice," he told her.

"Mama has come around a lot more lately. Seeing me dressed up like this," Lexi twirled playfully, "it seemed to lighten her spirits."

He grinned watching her spin. "I think you would light up any room just by walking into it."

She gasped and stood there looking at him. "What?" She whispered.

He stepped closer toward her with a small grin. "You have this way about you of being free. No matter what is bothering you, no matter what has happened in your life, you have this way of lighting up people around you. It makes you beautiful."

She stood there, speechless, having no idea what to say. Her lips parted and a small squeak erupted.

He chuckled and stepped closer toward her. His hand reached next to her, as if he were to lean in to use his truck as support. Instead, the truck door unlatched.

She exhaled a breath she'd been holding then lowered her gaze. Was it foolish of her to think he would kiss her just then? Well, he was going to the other night. "Thank you," she finally whispered.

He touched her chin and lifted her face up. He smiled down at her, and winked. "You never have to thank me for compliments like that. You deserve them." He then leaned in and pressed a soft kiss on her lips.

She kissed him back and her stomach fluttered. More than anything, she wanted to pull him close, like she did in the water.

He pulled away first and took a step back. "Your ride awaits."

She nodded then stepped toward the truck. As she was about to step inside, she quickly turned to face him. She cupped his face and quickly kissed him. Her lips remained on his for a moment, then, as she pulled away, she remained close enough that she could feel his breath fanning on her skin. "You deserved that kiss... and, I feel, many more." She looked up into his eyes and watched as his lips pulled into a smile.

"I'm very happy to hear that."

She smiled again, turned, and climbed into his truck.

Robert caught a glimpse of her thigh and grinned. Hell, he had seen her in her bra and panties already at the cliffs, but this was different. This was a date. He closed the door, then walked around, and got inside, starting it up. "How are you with dancing?"

"Oh, I can cut a rug or two," she replied. Lexi crossed her legs toward him then gazed over. "How about you cowboy, you dance?"

He put the truck into gear and backed down the driveway enough to turn it around. "I'll have you know my mother made me take dance lessons as a child. I have a mean Rumba, can Salsa, and I also Swing dance."

"Oh I've done died and gone to girly girl heaven!" She laughed and relaxed next to him. "Then I'll be happy to let you lead because honestly, around here? Mostly all we do is line dance. That shit gets boring after a while. No one dances very well from what I've experienced. But then again, maybe you'll prove me wrong tonight!"

"Damn straight, I will." He smirked and turned on the stereo. "Feel free to put it on whatever you like. I listen to just about anything... well except rap. I'm not much into that."

She smiled and recognized the satellite stations. She switched it to the Hits One stations and sat back.

He looked over to her then back to the road. "Well, I surely didn't ping you for this type of music." He laughed. "But hey, I'm cool."

"I bet you thought I'd put on some old George Strait and sing *All My Ex's Live In Texas*, didn't you?"

"Is that a joke? Because all your ex's do live in Texas."

She smiled then dropped her gaze. She immediately thought of Blaine. "Well, not all of them, I guess."

"I'm sorry, Lexi. I didn't mean to..."

"No, it's fine." She cut him off and smiled. "Really, it's okay. We're over, he's my ex, and hell he's from here!" She grinned. "So, where are you taking me?"

He had regretted the joke as soon as he'd told it. The look in her eyes told him the memory was still there and ever so fresh. He pulled up to a light and looked over at her. "Well, I thought it would be fun to go to the chop house in town."

"Oh, Shyanne's! Yeah that place is great! You know they moved the restaurant up top and made the original ground floor a dance floor?" She smiled and Robert relaxed seeing the excitement in her face.

"No, I didn't know that." He grinned then drove when the light turned green. "Sounds perfect, then." He winked at her and continued down the road. He pulled into the parking lot and noticed how full it was. "You're alright with waiting?"

"Sure. I'll be with you." She smiled and lowered her gaze. "You don't mind waiting with me?"

"Not in the least."

She looked up into his eyes and smiled. He wanted to lean across the truck and kiss her, have a full on make out session with her. Instead, the dome light came on when she pulled on the door handle. He inhaled and sighed, then stepped out.

Robert went to take Lexi's hand, then changed his mind and raised it to the back of his neck. She looked up at him with a curious gaze. He grinned, then lowered his hand and decided the small of her back was enough... for now.

~

*T*he hostess greeted them and she looked Robert over a few times. "Bobby Ray Shaw? Is that you?"

Lexi smiled then turned to him. "Bobby Ray, this is Estelle Chaplin. Estelle, you remember Bobby Ray." She smiled at the woman then shifted her gaze back to him with playful look.

"Pleasure to meet you, again, I think?" He smiled and stepped closer to Lexi. "Table for two, please."

"Yes, sir, right away." Estelle smiled and he noticed she had a gold cap on her front tooth and her hair looked frizzed, maybe from the humidity. He raised a brow when she turned away from them, then looked at Lexi.

She shook her head as if telling him, *not now.*

Estelle escorted the two of them to a table near a dark corner, and laid out the menus. "The special tonight is Sirloin steak and sweet potato. Enjoy, you two!" Estelle winked at Robert, then turned and walked away.

He noticed she tried to put a little extra swing in her step. She turned once and looked back at him. Robert immediately shifted his gaze to Lexi and smiled. "Well, that was interesting."

"Umm, Estelle didn't exactly… do well after high school." Lexi opened her menu and pretended to look it over. She then leaned toward him, as if blocking her conversation from the world by the menu in her hands. "She got heavy into drugs and other stuff. Word has it her old man is in the pen."

"Her old man?" He asked and leaned into her menu with her. He smelled her perfume and allowed it to tease his senses. *Damn, she looked good tonight. That dress is amazing on her body.*

"Yeah, her, umm, baby daddy?"

Robert chuckled. "Baby daddy? Nice Lexi." He sat back up and shook his head. "Well, at least she's working. So what's good here?" He quickly changed the subject, not wanting their first date to be focused on a woman who had made wrong decisions in life.

"The sirloin is really good. So is the barbeque chicken."

The two continued to look through their menu when their waitress walked up. She introduced herself as Starla. "What can I get ya to drink?" She looked between the two of them.

Lexi looked at Robert and raised her brows. "Well," she turned back to the waitress, "I'll start with a Hurricane, and a glass of ice water."

"Yes ma'am, just need to see your ID."

Lexi nodded and pulled out her driver's license, handing it over. The waitress glanced at it then handed it back. Robert ordered a Corona. Starla wrote it down then said she'd be back for their orders.

Out of ear shot, Lexi leaned over again. "I wonder why she didn't ask you for your ID?"

He grinned. "Because I look over twenty-one, I suppose." He winked and leaned in. "You continue to lean in like this I'll be left with no choice but to kiss you."

"Oh," she quickly sat up and blush ran over her face.

Robert chuckled. "Well, that wasn't me trying to get rid of you. I was only giving you a fair warning."

She nodded. "Fair enough. But if you'll excuse me, I need to find the ladies room."

He stood with her and when she walked away, he sat back down and watched her walk away. He shook his head and smiled.

He began looking over his menu again when suddenly a pair of lips was at his ear. Her perfume was light but her scent was alluring. Her hair tumbled down her shoulders onto his own. "Order me the sirloin, medium, with a sweet potato if she comes back before I get back." Lexi then kissed his ear. She quickly pulled away and walked toward the bathroom.

Robert's head jerked up and watched her, having no idea she had even come back. "Damn, she's good."

As the door closed behind her, Lexi took a deep breath to calm her beating heart. She stepped closer toward the bathroom sink and looked to herself in the mirror.

"It's just a casual date. We're here to have fun." She swallowed hard and found she had a hard time breathing.

"Honey, are you okay?"

Lexi looked over at a waitress who was standing beside her. Her hair was pulled to the nape of her neck and a hair band surrounded her head. She blinked, watching Lexi for a moment.

"Umm, yes, I'm fine. Thank you." She looked down at the sink and turned it on. The cold water ran over her hands and offered small relief to the heat she was feeling in her body.

"First date jitters?"

"Something like that."

"Is he cute?" The waitress grinned at Lexi in the mirror.

"He's very cute, like super cute. He's hot." Lexi blushed.

"Then what's the problem?"

Lexi turned to the woman, unsure of how they ended up in this conversation. Having no idea who she was, she felt she had nothing to lose. *Not like I'll see her again,* she told herself. "I just broke up with my boyfriend. The guy I'm here with is only here for the summer."

The woman smiled. "Then what's the problem?"

"I'm scared, I guess."

"Well? When you're done eating, go for a dance. Test him out on the floor. If he's worth dancing with he's worth a second date." The woman nodded to Lexi then turned to walk out. "Good luck," she called.

"Thanks," Lexi whispered.

Lexi went back to the table and slid into her seat. He watched her the entire time, taking a pull on his beer. When she looked up at him, he grinned. "You took me by surprise, you know?"

She laughed. "I like to keep you on your toes." She took a drink from her Hurricane. "Mmm it's good. Wanna try?"

He shook his head. "You most certainly did. I quite enjoyed it.

And no thanks, I'm good." He reached over for her hand, putting behind him any issues of ex-boyfriends and their summer ending. He intended to have fun with Lexi tonight.

Starla returned with their food and laid out two steaks with sweet potatoes. "If there's anything else you need, I'll be around shortly."

They nodded and began to eat.

During the course of their meal, they discussed his college career, what she was studying in large equine medicine and the events Robert had attended with his stepfather.

"My mother is very happy, which, honestly, is a far cry from where she was when she left my father. I remember how much she hated living here, hated being married to him and I remember watching my life leave out the back window of her car."

"Oh, Bobby Ray, I'm so sorry." She squeezed his hand, offering comfort. "It seems all has worked out for you now though, right? You seem happy."

He was happy, wasn't he? He had everything he could want back home in Georgia. He had his school, his mom and stepdad, and he had his friends and the occasional date. He looked Lexi over and gave himself a moment before he answered.

She wondered if he heard her. As she was about to speak up, he shifted in his seat, and she decided to wait.

"Well, I have pretty much everything I want, yes. But not everything I might need." His thumb gently ran over the back of her hand.

She held her breath for a moment before she lowered her gaze. In her entire time with Blaine, he had never talked to her like this. It was always about his music, getting signed, and getting the hell out of Dodge. Looking back on it, she believed he never intended for her to be part of his future. She turned away from Robert for a moment and removed her hand.

"What's the matter? Did I say something wrong?" He asked her.

"Hardly," she scoffed. "If anything, you're saying all the right things." She looked over and glared at him. "Why? Why are you here with me? Why are you doing this?"

"Whoa, wait, what? What am I doing? I'm not sure I understand."

"You told me yourself that you're leaving at the end of summer. You told me you didn't want to become serious, you know, just be friends."

"Yeah?" He answered.

"Then why do this? Why go through all the trouble of trying to flatter me when it's all for nothing?" She sat back in her chair and folded her arms over her chest.

He raised his brows, having no idea where this outburst was coming from. He watched her for a moment and considered a different approach. "If this is about Blaine, I'm not him."

"It's obvious you're not him." She turned and glared at him.

"Then what's the problem? I fail to see what I did wrong here."

"That's it right there!" Her voice began to rise.

He shook his head, still not getting it. "What is? Help me understand." He kept himself calm and at the same time, felt something inside of him want to yell out for her to cut the shit... that he wanted to be with her. But did he? He was leaving, like she said.

"Bobby Ray, really?" She looked over to him. "You are saying and doing all the right things to woo me."

"Woo you?" He raised his brows and tried not to smile.

"YES! Woo me!" She huffed and turned away from him. "And dammit, it's working, okay? You're leaving and... and..." She stopped and sat there, not saying anything else.

Robert stood up from his chair and ran his hand down his face. Since they were done with their dinner, he felt it was time to change the scenery. He walked around in front of her and offered his hand.

"What are you doing?" She looked up at him.

He saw her eyes wet with threatening tears. "Well, if you'll take my hand, you'll find out."

She shook her head and looked away.

"Lexi, come on. Take my hand. Don't make me beg, because I have no shame in begging. I'll get down on my damn knees and cry out for you to take my hand."

She gasped and looked back at him. "You wouldn't!"

"Oh I most certainly would!" He grinned and began to get down on one knee.

She immediately put her hand in his. "My god, don't do that!"

He helped her stand and gave her a lop-sided grin.

She found herself smiling and shook her head. "Okay, now what?"

"Let me lead and you follow. Remember?" He offered more of a smile, softening his face. He saw reluctance in her response, but she followed him nonetheless.

He led her down the stairs to the dance floor. The song ended and *To Make You Feel My Love* began to play. He led her out to the dance floor, and turned her to face him. He placed his hand on her waist and took her hand.

She rested her hand on his shoulder.

He led her in a slow two-step, keeping his eyes on hers. The first few steps he felt her rigid body. "Relax," he told her.

"I'm trying," she replied.

His fingers spread across her back and he pulled her closer to him. His head leaned in and his cheek touched hers.

Her hand moved up around his neck and she began to press her body against his. She relaxed more into his hold as they danced.

"You are the most beautiful, most caring woman I've met in a long time." He whispered into her ear. "You carry so much on your shoulders, yet you seem free. It's as if nothing can hinder you. Even with me, you see me, not the person everyone else sees.

This is what attracts me to you. You're like my light in a dark tunnel."

Her arm tightened around his neck. He pulled her hand in and rested it above his heart, holding her closer. Their steps were small as they danced together.

She raised her gaze up to his and looked into his eyes. "You have no idea how much what you said means to me."

"I can only guess." He smiled.

The song ended and their eyes remained on each other's. At the last chord, he stopped, cupped her face, and kissed her. It was soft, sweet, and not rushed.

A few whoops and hollers sounded when the tempo changed to Toby Keith. She pulled away from the kiss first and her eyes remained closed for a moment.

He was concerned he had crossed the line when she wouldn't look at him, then a smile formed on her lips. Lexi's eyes opened, and she smiled.

He grinned and chuckled. "Come on, let's swing."

"I don't know how!" She laughed when he took her hands.

"You don't need to. I'll lead you."

The two danced through a few more songs with a few different dance styles. Checking the time, Lexi smiled and let go of Robert.

"It's getting late. I work tomorrow and need to get some sleep."

"Ahh, yes, ma'am. Well, let's get on out and get you settled." He winked then took her hand in his. He lifted their hands and kissed her fingers. "Thank you for an amazing night."

She smiled and tilted her head slightly. "It's not over yet."

He grinned wider before he leaned in and kissed her. *I Love This Bar* came on and Robert chuckled. "Yeah, it's time to go."

She nodded with a laugh. They headed toward the exit and walked out, not suspecting they were being watched.

Abby Masters stood in the darkened bar, by the dance floor,

and watched the two of them leave. She pulled out her phone and sent a message to Blaine.

You need to hurry up and get back here. For one, I miss you. Another, she's kissing all over that Bobby Ray.

She pressed send and pocketed her phone, then turned back to the man who was buying her drinks. "What did you say your name was, Sugar?"

CHAPTER 6

*R*obert pulled up to Lexi's home and put the Dually into park. The night sky was dark and the stars were out. He reached over and turned down the radio, then looked over at her.

Lexi slipped off her seat belt and sat there for a moment. "Robert," she started.

"Robert? What happened to Bobby Ray?" He grinned.

She looked up and smiled. "Well, Robert is a man's name. And tonight, you've been more of a man to me, than he ever was."

He kept his eyes on hers, knowing *he* meant Blaine. "Lexi…"

"No please, let me say this." She scooted across the seat toward him until their knees touched. "I had a great time tonight. I didn't think about anything but you and the fun we were having. Then, when you kissed me…" She trailed off and inched closer to him.

Robert swallowed and listened to her. She moved her hand to his thigh and he quickly inhaled. "Lexi…" He looked into her eyes and removed his cowboy hat, setting it on the dashboard. He ran his hand through his hair, never once breaking eye contact.

"Kiss me," she whispered. "Please."

He touched her cheek and allowed his fingers to graze down

to her jawline. He skimmed his nails over her neckline, to her collarbone. He listened to her inhale a sharp breath at his touch. He reached over with his other hand and cupped her cheek. He tilted her head up then leaned in and captured her lips.

A sigh left her lips as she kissed him back. Her hands moved to his chest and her fingers tensed until they tightened into his shirt.

He felt her pull him closer to her. He titled his head the other way and deepened the kiss. When she whimpered against his lips, he pulled away just enough to catch his breath. "Damn woman..."

She smiled and tilted her head up, catching his lips again. Her tongue swiped his lips and she giggled when he growled against hers. This time she pulled away, then rested her forehead against his. "Damn is right," she breathed.

"What time you getting off tomorrow? Because we're picking up where we left off here."

She laughed and pulled away enough to look into his eyes. "Are you sweet on me, Bobby Ray?"

"Maybe," he chuckled when she called him by his nickname. He found himself growing used to the nickname and didn't mind it in the least.

～

*T*he next day, Robert took himself to the tailors for his tuxedo fitting. The conversation over breakfast humored him.

"Rather than renting, I'd rather pay for one, if it's all the same to you," his father told him.

"Whatever you want Pop; it's your big day."

"Oh no honey, it's MY big day!" Sabrina laughed then kissed Robert's father.

He shook his head and left the house. His mind wandered to Lexi and he found himself smiling. Robert looked in the mirror and wanted to call himself a love struck fool. His mind also told him he's only here for the summer.

"Mr. Shaw, please raise your arms out to your sides."

Robert nodded and did as the tailor requested. He looked at himself in the mirror again and did a double take. "Lexi?" He turned and lowered his arms. He jumped off the pedestal and took off for the door.

"Mr. Shaw! Wait!" The tailor called.

"Just a minute, I'll be right back!" Robert ran out the door and caught up to her. "Lexi?"

She stopped and turned. She wore a pink and white halter-top with denim shorts, and white sandals. Her hair was pulled into a pony tail.

Lexi looked damn sexy. He wanted to pick her up and carry her inside, preferably to an empty room in the back. He wanted to kiss her again, however this time, not just on her lips.

She grinned when she saw him. "Wow, nice suit. Going somewhere fancy?"

He looked her over with a grin. "Oh you know, there's this wedding I'm in." He winked. "Why don't you come inside? I shouldn't be much longer."

"Oh, I don't want to impose." She folded her hands in front of her with a Cheshire grin.

"Oh no, you don't. Get in here, woman!" He took her hands and pulled her close, then kissed her.

She grinned against his lips and felt her stomach flip with butterflies. "I wouldn't pass up a fashion show put on by my own Bobby Ray Shaw!"

He noticed Lexi calling him hers. He grinned, "Well, I won't be walking any cat walks or anything if that's what you're thinking."

"Oh darn!" She feigned a pout then walked inside the tailors with him.

He introduced her as she took a seat. A seamstress stepped out and smiled at her. The older woman reminded her of her mother.

"Oh honey, you have the body of a model! You can wear anything and make it look good!"

Lexi blushed and smiled. "Wow, thank you so much! I don't think I do, but thank you."

"Oh, you most certainly do," Robert protested.

She looked up at him with raised brows.

"Shit!" He yelled out when the tailor ran the tape measure up his leg and touched his balls. "Dude, really?"

"My apologies, Mr. Shaw."

Lexi busted out laughing, then tried to hide her giggle behind her hands. The tailor smirked and continued to measure his legs.

A little while later, Robert put his regular clothes back on and went out to find Lexi. He walked up behind her and shifted her hair. He kissed her shoulder lightly. "Ready to go?"

She turned in his arms and found him wearing a University of Georgia t-shirt with a pair of tight fitted jeans and boots. She took him all in then nodded. "You realize you're wearing rival colors, right? Any Longhorn or Aggie fan around here will find you and accuse you of fighting words."

"Fighting words? Even when I haven't said anything?" He questioned her.

She nodded and rested her hands on his chest, allowing them to feel how strong... how thick his chest was. She felt herself melt just a little. "Mmhmm. Someone might accuse you of turning your back on your true colors."

"Oh... is that it?" He chuckled. "What do you suppose I do about it?"

She blushed slightly when she smiled. "Well, I'm going to find a dress. You can find another shirt if you want... or I suppose you could take your chances in asking for a fight."

"A dress? What's the occasion?" He reached up and shifted her hair from her face, then pushed it behind her ear. "I'll take my chances on my shirt."

"Suit yourself." She smiled. "Well, I have this date to a wedding with this really sweet, very good looking guy. I'd really like to look my best." She leaned into him as her breath fanned his lips. "And by best, I mean I want to look damn sexy."

His lips parted and he felt a twitch when his erection responded to her. "Is that so?" He leaned in a little closer and his nose skimmed hers.

She wrapped her arms around his waist and leaned back a little as he bent over her. A throat cleared next to them and Lexi looked over. "Oh," embarrassed, she pulled away and lowered her gaze. "Beg your pardon." She turned away from Robert and began to walk. She quickly turned back, "I'll, umm… meet you outside." She shifted on her feet then hurried toward the door.

Robert chuckled and shook his head. "What do I owe ya?" The tailor rang up his tuxedo and gave him the date it would be ready. Robert paid the deposit, pocketed the receipt, and turned toward the door. He heard the tailor mention something about a fine young honey. He couldn't agree more.

He found Lexi waiting outside for him and, when she looked over, she busted out laughing.

"Oh my god, that was so embarrassing!" She walked up to him and rested her forehead on his chest.

His arms went around her slender frame and he chuckled. "Nah, it's fine. Matter of fact, he called you a fine young honey."

She looked up with wide eyes. "He didn't!"

"He most certainly did." Robert smiled.

"Well," she started, a little teasing in her voice, "coming from a man who was obviously more into measuring your crotch than he was into checking me out… that's saying something." She pursed her lips to keep from laughing.

"Oh, is that what you're going with?" He laughed and shook his head.

She shrugged, "Yup!"

They walked down to the dress store a few doors down. He opened the door for her and walked inside. The cool air conditioning blew against their bodies as the door closed behind them. The store was small, privately owned.

Looking around, Robert raised his brows. "Well, I said I'd do this with you, but now... I don't know."

Bridesmaid's dresses, wedding gowns, and prom dresses hung on the racks and display windows. Lexi turned and looked at him with a raised brow. "Oh, come on, Bobby Ray. All you have to do is hold my purse." She grinned and waited for his response.

"It's a good thing I like you, woman or I wouldn't be doing this." He stepped farther into the store with a sigh. "Do I get to help you change?" He asked with raised brows and a smirk.

"Bobby Ray!" She playfully smacked his arm. "Absolutely not!" She gathered herself and stood straighter. "I might let you see the dresses though. She raised a brow. "If you're lucky, I might show you some leg."

"Woman," he stepped closer with a grin. "I've seen a lot more than your leg." He leaned in a little closer and inhaled, picking up the scent of her perfume. The light, floral fragrance suited her. "Cliff diving?" The memories of her body in her bra and panties surfaced to the forefront of his mind.

Her lips parted to protest then she closed them. "Fine, just for that, no leg." She turned on her heel and marched back toward the dressing room. She looked over her shoulder to see if he was following, then gave him a sly grin.

He raised his brows, then smiled and followed her. "Let me see you naked and I'll hold anything you want!" He chuckled with a wide smile.

"BOBBY RAY!" She exclaimed and turned to face him, her face as red as a ripe tomato.

"What? You're sexy woman. I want to see you naked!" He smirked and stepped closer toward her. "Don't tell me you don't fantasize about seeing me in my birthday suit." He looked into her eyes and as she gasped, he stepped closer, touching her cheek. "You gonna let me in there with you?" He grinned again.

"Sir, we do not condone that type of conduct in here!" A woman's voice came in from behind Robert.

He turned to look over his shoulder at her. She was tall and large. Her hair almost completely grayed, she had it pulled to the back of her head in a bun. Her dark blue dress gave her the appearance of a school teacher. "Yes, ma'am," he told her.

Lexi held her lips together to keep from laughing then ended up letting out a small snort. She covered her hands over her mouth just as Robert turned to look at her. "D-dresses?" She giggled then turned and headed away from the store clerk.

A short while later, Robert sat waiting in a chair outside the dressing rooms. He crossed his right ankle over his left knee then placed both hands under his head. He yawned, and his eyes moved about the store. He shook his head and thought, *if Mom could see me now.*

"Well?" Lexi stepped out of the dressing room with a calf length light pink dress. It was sleeveless and the neckline ran high. A white belt circled around her waist and she twirled in a circle. The bottom of the dress fanned out slightly.

Robert smiled and nodded. "Looks nice on you. I think something a little more... oh, I don't know, open? You know," he motioned over his chest with a wink.

She shook her head and laughed. "Right, of course you'd say that."

"I'm a guy! It's what I do, woman!" He watched her disappear back into the dressing room, and his phone buzzed. He pulled it out and saw Makayla's name flash on his screen. He swiped it and read her message.

Hey cuz! I hear you had a good date the other night with Lexi! What are your intentions with her? Because honestly, it sounds like you're becoming boyfriend material. Now I know it's not my business but she's one of my bestest friends. Please, don't hurt her and I don't want to see you hurt either. <3 you cuz. M.

He sighed and read the message again. He thought about replying to her, he also thought about just deleting her message. Instead, he shoved the phone back in his pocket when Lexi walked out again.

He smiled and nodded to her again. "Now, that's getting better."

"You think? This is more like a cocktail dress I think." She ran her hands down the black fabric and looked in the three-way mirror. The halter style dress fit Lexi's body like a glove; the hem hit just below her mid-thigh.

He stood up from his seat and walked up behind her. Robert looked over her with a hungry grin. "Wedding or not, damn you're getting that dress."

She turned around and looked up at him. Her cheeks pinked slightly and she smiled. "You like this, huh?" She lowered her gaze and pushed her hair behind her ear. "I feel so..."

"Sexy?" he finished for her. He lifted up her chin and looked into her eyes again.

"I was going to say exposed, but sexy works." She laid her hands on his chest, feeling the muscles under his shirt ripple.

"Exposed, you'd be naked." His voice was gruff and he leaned into her then kissed her lips. "I meant what I said, you're getting this dress," he mumbled against her lips.

She nodded then pulled away. "Let me go try on the last one," she said, putting a little space between them.

She ducked away into the dressing room and Robert adjusted himself. He looked around and found a few older women watching him. He smiled, and nodded to each of them. They smiled then turned about their on tasks.

He sat back down and relaxed, thinking of Lexi in that black dress. "Good night, I'm in a lot of trouble." He pulled his phone back out and looked at Makayla's message again. He hit reply and began.

Hey cuz. It's admirable you're looking out for her best interest, but trust me; you have nothing to worry about.

He hit send and pocketed his phone when he heard Lexi gasp. "You alright in there?" He called to her.

"Oh, I'm fine, thank you for asking." She answered with what sounded like a soft laugh in her voice.

Robert shook his head and sighed. Lexi came back out of the dressing room, holding two dresses and wearing the clothes she came in with. "What about the other dress? Because I'm gonna tell you now. You wear that black one; you'll be showing up the bride." He grinned.

"You're so sweet!" She hung the black dress over the other one on her arm, making it obvious she was trying to conceal it. "I don't want you to see what I'm getting. I want it to be a surprise. Trust me; it's perfect!"

He raised his brows. "Alright, then. Well, let's get this paid for and get outta here. I'm hungry and you, darlin', are my date." They walked up to the counter and Lexi laid the dresses down. Robert pulled out his wallet and as Lexi was about to protest, he held up his hand to her. "No, please, this is my treat. I asked you to be my date to my father's wedding. Allow me to do this for you."

"It's not necessary," she told him in a softer voice.

He reached for her hand and pulled it to his lips. He kissed the back of her hand and watched her for a moment. "I know it's not, but I want to do this." She hesitated for another moment then finally nodded.

～

*R*iding in their tour bus, Blaine placed ointment over a new tattoo he'd had put on the night before. Completing a sleeve on his left arm, he looked over the detail of the work. At one point, he had a heart on his bicep with Latin inscribed inside it, *Catapultam Habeo Liberum*. And next to it, Lexi's initials.

"Love Conquers All baby. That's us." At least, that's what he told her.

Fucking, Music, and Freedom is what it actually meant. She'd never taken Latin so how would she know? Then again, neither did he.

"That could say General Tsao's Chicken for all you know!" His drummer yelled in a fit of laughter.

Blaine picked up a roll of paper towels nearby and threw them toward his head. The others sitting nearby chuckled.

Since leaving Texas and experiencing said freedom, Blaine covered the tattoo up with different tribal markings and a naked female demon complete with horns and her tongue sticking out.

He laid a bandage over the area to protect it then pulled out his phone. He scrolled through a few images of the women he'd captured in his bed with a smirk. Some were tall, some were short. Some were rail thin, others were fit. Since being on tour, the women would line up to get a glance at his band... and him. A country boy from Texas who turned to rock music... who knew? Well, he knew, and he also knew remaining home in Texas with Lexi on his arm would only hold him back.

Of course, when it came to Lexi, he enjoyed having her on the other end of things. She followed him around like a lost puppy dog. She held onto every word, had been at every practice, and would follow him to the ends of the earth.

Blaine? Not so much. He was her first love, first sexual experience... first everything. He'd intended to be her last until his band got good. Like... really good. So good they were signed shortly after he graduated high school. They only had to replace the drummer, which he hadn't been too heartbroken over.

"Nah, Jimmy will find a gig somewhere else. We don't need him anyway," he told his bandmates.

Of course, they all disagreed at the time until they met Matt, their newest drummer. He was like hell on wheels when it came to drumming. Letting go of Jimmy had been exactly what they needed and Blaine was never ashamed to admit as much.

While scrolling through his pictures, he came across an old photo of Lexi. She stood in her swimsuit, her skin was tan, and she was smiling. He then expanded the picture and zoomed in on her breasts. They were perky and fucking perfect.

He shook his head and rubbed his crotch. "Damn, bitch still gets me hard," he mumbled.

"What's that?" Matt called. The drummer sat across the bus while beating on the seat in front of him.

"Nothing man, just reminiscing."

Matt stood and came across the bus, then sat next to Blaine. "Damn, who's the hottie? She's got amazing tits."

"Hey now, that's my girl," Blaine told him then pocketed his phone. "Show a little respect."

"You're kidding, right? Your girl? You got a damn different bitch each show. How is she your girl? She knows what it's like on the road, right?"

"Oh yeah, sure. She's cool," he said, then looked out the window. "Well, she will be if she knows what's good for her."

"Ahh man, you need to do that girl a favor and let her go. This isn't the life for her. If you're fucking around..."

Blaine cut him off. "Ain't your business, man." He turned and glared at the drummer.

"It's cool, just saying, do her a favor. That's all." Matt stood and returned to his seat. He pulled out sheet music and pulled on headphones. He glanced back at Blaine then shook his head. He turned back and began beating on the seat again.

CHAPTER 7

*R*obert came down the stairs in his dad's home and found Sabrina in the kitchen preparing dinner. He snagged a fry off the paper towel and she slapped his hand. "Manners, Bobby Ray!"

"Wow, you, too? Does no one want to call me Robert?" He smiled then ate the fry. "Mmm perfect."

"Thank you. If you're looking for your dad, he's outside." She turned back to the fryer.

"Actually, no. I was coming down to talk to you." He leaned against the counter and watched her turn the country style potatoes.

She sat down the spatula then wiped her hands on a towel. "Okay, what can I help you with?"

"Well," he sighed and grabbed the back of his neck. "It's Lexi."

"Mmmhmm, you like her, don't you?" She smiled.

"Yeah, I do. She's great and she deserves greatness. I'm afraid that's just it. I don't think I'm the one to give it to her."

"Why not? Why couldn't you?"

"Well, because for one, I live in Georgia and am in college. I'm starting my senior year there soon…"

She cut him off. "Bullshit. Give me a real reason why you couldn't."

He looked up with a start. "What do you mean? And so you know, that IS a real reason." He furrowed his brows.

"No, it's an excuse. You want the truth? I'll give it to you. It's a quality your father admires in me. I don't hold back and I tell it like it is." She turned to the potatoes and flipped them over before wiping her hands again. "Now you listen to me, Robert." Her using his birth name didn't go unnoticed. "If you like this girl, and I mean, really like her, then you need to do the honorable thing and tell her. You need to make something of it and not just lead her on.

"Eventually the two of you will build feelings and it'll be more than a damn summer fling. You need to really consider what she means to you, and what you mean to her." She raised one brow. "Makayla filled us in when I asked about her." She held up her hand to Robert when was about to speak. "No, honey, let me finish. I may not be your mother, but I do care about you and your feelings. I know you're headed back to Georgia at the end of summer, but I also know what it's like to have a broken heart."

Robert nodded then waited to see if she was finished. Satisfied, he began. "I appreciate all of that, I really do. I know you were there for Pop when Mom left him. I know you were there to pick up the pieces and honestly, I have no idea what he would have done if it hadn't been for you."

Sabrina smiled and patted Robert's arm. "Honey, this isn't about me and your father."

"I know it's not, but you have to put yourself in my place for a moment."

"Why? You like her don't you?" she asked.

He nodded. "Yeah, she's amazing. She's fun, kind, considerate, and she calls me on my bullshit. Hell, she did it the other night!" Robert chuckled.

"Then transfer schools. UTA, TCU, and SMU all have great

education programs. There's no reason you can't finish up here and study whatever you want to do with families."

"It's not that easy," he said. Robert looked out the window and watched his father as he dusted off his hands. He laid work gloves on the table outside and began walking toward the house.

"Yes, it is that easy. Go to the university here, whichever one that is, register, then have your transcripts sent over. Done." She turned back to the potatoes and placed them onto the paper towel. "Now, if you'll excuse me, I need to finish up dinner for me and your father. You're welcome to join us and this conversation never happened." She looked up to him and winked.

"Thank you, Sabrina. I appreciate that." He leaned in and kissed her cheek. "You've been real good for my Pop. You've earned your keep here." He smiled then turned to leave as his father walked through the door.

"Hey son, where you headed?" He shut the door then winked at Sabrina.

"Dinner's almost ready," she told him.

"Smells great, baby." He then looked over at Robert as he walked out of the room.

"Got a date with a hot lady! Don't wait up!" Robert yelled back as he headed back up to his room.

He closed his bedroom door and walked to his closet. He looked over his clothes and thought about Sabrina's words on transferring schools, being here with Lexi, and seeing where things might go.

Leaving Georgia, he'd never seen Lexi coming. She was like a whirlwind... an erotic force of sexual tension that blows across your body. As soon as her scent is inhaled, her essence captivates you, and that's it; you're done.

He sighed and let his head drop until his chin touched his chest. "Dammit. Well, it's only the end of June." He looked up at his polos and went to reach for one, then changed his mind. He reached for a button down black dress shirt and pulled it down. He looked it over and grinned.

He turned and walked back toward his bedroom door and yelled downstairs. "Excuse me, Sabrina? Do you iron with starch?"

~

"*Y*es Makayla, I really do like him! He's so nice, and damn, is he sexy!" Lexi laughed and fell back onto her bed. She lay against her cell phone on her pillow and sighed. "He's so nice and girl, he kisses so good!"

"Eww, okay I don't need to hear that part!" Makayla told her. "So, does this mean you're over scumbag?"

She turned onto her back and grabbed her phone. "Yes. No. Oh, I don't know!" She folded her free arm over her eyes. "I guess so."

"Umm, no. You need to KNOW so, Lexi. Don't mess with his heart like that, okay?"

"Yes, ma'am," she told her. "I didn't intend to have anything other than a friendship with him. I mean it! I really didn't. You're my best friend and I'm going to be completely honest with you. I thought... well? He'd be like a rebound." She held her breath for a second. "I think we both thought that. But after the other night... even earlier dress shopping..."

She trailed off and Makayla giggled into the phone. "You took him dress shopping with you?"

"Well, sort of. I was walking down the street and he saw me while getting fitted for his tuxedo. Oh Makayla, he looked so hot!"

She sighed into the phone. "Really, Lexi?" Sarcasm was thick in her voice. "I don't need to hear that. So what happened?"

Lexi went into the details on how Robert pulled her into the store, giggled through how the tailor reached between his legs. Makayla laughed hard into the phone. When they both recovered,

Lexi told her about Robert going dress shopping with her. "Makayla, he bought my dresses."

"Dresses? Like more than one?"

"Uh huh. More than one. I tried on this one dress, this black one. It was fitted and I swear to you, Bobby Ray was going to strip me then and there!" She whispered into the phone, "He said he wanted to see me naked!"

"Oh my GAWD, Lexi!" Makayla busted out laughing.

"What's so damn funny?"

"Nothing, just… nothing!" She giggled a little more.

"Okay fine. Whatever. It's NOT funny!" She sat on her bed and made a pouty face.

"Oh c'mon! It IS funny! The fact you whispered it to me when no one is home with you, yeah, that's funny!"

"Oh whatever! I'm done with you! Good bye!"

Makayla laughed again. "Oh, okay, I love you. Be good!"

She sighed and shook her head. "I love you. Bye." Lexi hung up the phone and tossed it on her bed. She shook her head and let out a soft laugh, then stood. She made her way to the dresses that hung in front of her closet. She ran her hand over the fabric of the black dress and stared at it. "What am I going to do with you?"

Her phone rang again. She walked back to her bed and without looking at the screen, she answered. "I don't want to talk to you. I'm still mad at you for laughing at me. And whatever, he's hot, okay?"

"Umm, who's hot?" Robert asked.

"Oh shit, Bobby Ray?" Lexi pulled her phone back and stared at his name. Her face immediately heated from embarrassment and she slowly pulled the phone back. "Umm… no one?"

"So, no one is hot? And who are you mad at?" He smiled into the phone and turned down the road toward her house.

"Well, you know what? It doesn't matter," she said matter-of-factly.

"If you say so." He chuckled. "I'll be there in about ten minutes. You ready to head out on our date?"

"Umm, well, not quite."

"I can't wait to see you in that black dress again, Lexi." He growled into the phone.

She felt herself swoon and her knees weaken. She closed her eyes and leaned against the wall, trying not to breathe heavily into the phone.

"Lexi?"

"Umm," she straightened herself. "Yeah I'm here." She pulled the dress down and held onto it as if it were some kind of hot acid. She shook her head. "Robert..."

He felt it. He knew something was wrong. "Lexi, it's okay, you don't have to..."

"No, it's not that," she started. "I'll wear it, but not tonight, okay? I'm not... I don't think..."

"Lexi, I promise, it's okay. Wear whatever you like tonight. It's perfectly fine. I promise." He had his answer right then. She wasn't ready for him, and who knew if she ever would be. He didn't want to push it because he was leaving in less than two months. Then again, every bit of him wanted to claim her as his.

"Are you sure? I don't want to disappoint you."

He could hear the sadness and maybe the desperation in her voice. "I promise, it's fine. I'll be there in a few minutes. Boots and jeans are good. Matter of fact," he began mentally changing their plans in his head. "Let's go to the rodeo tonight. I saw one adver-tised in the paper this morning.

She smiled with a sigh of relief. "Oh yeah! I saw that! The managers came by the tack store the other day gathering up equipment. It'll be fun!" She hung the dress back up and felt relieved to get it out of her grasp. As much as she enjoyed kissing Bobby Ray, at the same time, she wasn't sure she was ready to go to the next level... even if that was just making out.

"Perfect. Alright woman, see you shortly."

"Bye, Bobby Ray." She hung up and set her phone on her dresser. She pulled out a pair of tight fitted Wranglers, her red boots, red button down sleeveless blouse and grabbed her straw hat.

She went into her bathroom and ran her flat iron through her hair once more, then pulled on her shirt, buttoning it up to just above her bust line. She sprayed her perfume and walked through it, pulled on her jeans and boots, then her hat. She looked herself over with a nod, and headed downstairs.

Robert picked her up and they headed out to the arena near Fort Worth. He parked and glanced over at her with a smile. "Damn Lexi, you make casual look hot. You realize that, right?"

She smiled and gave him a shrug. "I aim to please," she said with a wink.

Robert climbed out of the truck then walked around to her side, opening her door. As she slid to the edge of the seat, he took her by the waist and helped her to the ground.

"It's not that far a distance from the running board to the ground, you know," she told him.

"I know. I would just have hated to have you hurt if you turned your ankle. I need to keep you safe." He winked at her and she smiled. He touched her chin and tilted her head up. "Have fun tonight. Don't worry about anything else."

The insinuation was in his voice and she heard it. She nodded and offered another smile.

He removed his hat, then leaned in, and kissed her softly. "You smell good, damn girl."

She grinned. "Thank you. Now, let's go watch the show." She placed her hand in his and gave it a squeeze.

He nodded and they headed toward the gates. Robert pulled out his wallet and paid the entrance fee. They took seats near the center of the arena. Riders were in the arena with their horses as they pranced with the American and Texas flag. They went in and out of formation as Robert and Lexi looked on.

The announcer came on and began calling out the order of events for the evening. Lexi leaned over to Robert, "I used to barrel race and steer undecorated."

"Really?" He looked into her eyes.

"Yeah, I stopped after high school," she shrugged. "I found no reason to keep it up other than just for fun. College happened and Blaine kept me busy all the time with his music shit."

"Music shit?" He asked with raised brows.

"Yeah, music shit. I wasted a few years of my life on that fucker." She sat back and crossed her arms over her chest. "If I knew then what I know now…"

"You'd do things differently?"

"Hell, yeah I would. I wouldn't have been so available."

He considered her words for a moment and thought about how to approach this subject. "You wouldn't let yourself be so available again?"

"Not in a million years." She kept her gaze on the arena.

Robert sat back in his chair and looked down at his hands. "Lexi…" he glanced over at her. "I'm not him. I would never treat you that way."

"Oh, Bobby Ray!" She exclaimed and turned to him. "I didn't mean you, honey; I know that! I only meant…"

"No, it's okay. I knew what you meant."

"Are you sure you do?" She raised a brow to him. "Because I don't think you do."

"No, I do. I've had my heart broken, too. Once, really badly. It hurt like hell, but I got over it. For a while, I compared the women I saw to her, thought they'd do the same thing she did. In the end, I let it go when I realized they wouldn't."

She looked him over for a moment then stood. "I'll be right back. I need to go to the bathroom."

"Alright, I'll be here." He watched her as she walked past. He sighed and wondered if he crossed any boundaries. He crossed his ankle over his leg and watched the little boys and girls during the mutton-bustin' event. The sheep were no match for the kids. As bothered as he was at their conversation, he found himself smiling. He thought it would be fun to one day be out here with his son or daughter and teach them how to ride the fearsome sheep.

He sat back in his seat as child after child rode out into the arena. Lexi hadn't returned and he looked toward the end of the aisle. She'd been gone a good twenty minutes by now. He stood and set out to find her.

$\mathcal{T}$he warm summer night air blew around Lexi's exposed arms. The fresh smell of hay filled her nose as she stood outside, near the stalls. Cowboys were running their hands on the rosin as they worked their ropes for their next ride.

"Am I making a mistake?" Lexi asked.

"I don't know, honey. What's your heart telling you?" Her mother asked.

She sighed into the phone. "To leap."

"Okay, then maybe you should. But before you do, consider how it will feel when he goes back to Georgia. Has he said anything about staying in Texas? Or maybe taking you with him?"

"Mama, I couldn't leave you. It's not even an option." Lexi leaned against the wall and wrapped her free arm around her waist.

"Yes, it is. I'll be fine if you go. You know that."

"Mama, no…" She stopped when she looked up and found Robert watching her. "Mama, I need to go. He's staring at me."

Her mother laughed. "Okay honey, good luck. Follow your heart."

"Okay, Mama. I love you." She hung up then pocketed her

phone. Lexi looked at the ground then pushed off the wall. She took a deep breath and looked up at Robert.

He stepped closer and kept his eyes on hers. He didn't say anything, he just stood there for a moment, and then he opened his arms.

She stared at him for a moment and her bottom lip began to tremble. She walked toward him and leaned into his embrace.

Robert wrapped his arms around her body and held her close. "I'm not going anywhere," he told her.

"Not yet, you're not," she told him. She looked up at him and blinked her tears away. "What happens when you do go?"

"What makes you think I'm going anywhere?" He smiled down at her.

She blinked, not understanding. "But after summer?"

"School starts up. I know." He smiled. "There are more schools than just in Georgia you know." He couldn't believe he had just said these words. Did he mean it or was he trying to keep her calm? He honestly did not know himself.

"Bobby Ray, you don't have to do this for me."

"There's a lot I'd do for you, Lexi. I just need to know if you'd be willing to do the same for me." Her brows rose in alarm and he shook his head. "I'm not asking for an answer, woman." He chuckled. "I'm only saying... you know? It doesn't matter. Let's go enjoy the show, okay?"

She nodded. "Okay." She leaned into his embrace again and tightened her arms around his waist.

He really enjoyed holding her like this. He thought for a moment of having her in his bed and sleeping next to her, waking up next to her, making love to her and amazing make up sex. He sighed and began to turn. "C'mon beautiful, let's go."

As they turned to walk back toward their seats, they heard a girl yell out. Lexi turned in time to find a horse get spooked. It came running toward them. Before she realized what was about to happen, the horse jumped, then kicked, landing a hoof in her side. Lexi dropped to the ground and curled on her side, groaning out loud

Robert yelled out and everything happened so fast. The woman on the horse was thrown off and rodeo clowns came running over in an effort to diffuse the situation.

Someone grabbed the reins of the horse and got him under control. The rider stood and came running over to Lexi's side. Robert yelled out for a medic and the ambulance was on its way.

"Holy shit, I'm so sorry! Damn livestock spooked my Bear! Is she okay? Oh hell, I hope nothing is broken!"

"I don't know," Robert told her. "Go get the ambulance over here, now!" He pulled the hat off Lexi's head and held her head in his hands. "Lexi, can you hear me? Talk to me, baby."

"Baby?" She groaned. "Did you call me baby?" She opened her eyes and looked up at Robert.

He smiled. "That I did. Can you breathe okay?"

"It hurts, but yeah, I can." She tried to touch her side then gasped.

"Don't do that; let the medic take a look. Where's your phone? I'll call your mama."

She pointed to where her phone was. He reached into her pocket for it. "Don't get frisky, Bobby Ray."

"Damn, you found me out." He winked at her. "What's your Mom under, oh never mind. Mom is pretty clear." He smiled and pressed dial.

The line picked up and a female voice answered. "Hey, honey. So did you tame that good looking man?"

"Umm... Mrs. Griffin? This is Robert Shaw."

"Oh, my gosh, how embarrassing! Wait. Did something happen to Lexi? Is she okay?"

"She will be, yes. We're on our way to the hospital." The medic told him Harris and he repeated this to Lexi's mother. "She was kicked by a spooked horse, ma'am. The ambulance is taking her now. I'll be riding in the ambulance with her."

"Oh Robert, thank you so much! I'll be there soon. Your name is Robert? She calls you Bobby Ray."

"Does she now? So your daughter talks about me?" He glanced over at Lexi and watched her eyes widen in shock and her face turn red. He chuckled.

"Well, I can see without even being there, she's close to you. Treat my baby good, Robert. Or you'll deal with me, understand?"

He smiled into the phone. "Yes ma'am. I plan on it."

"Good boy. Alright, I'll be at the hospital soon. Thank you for calling me."

"Yes ma'am." Robert hung up then walked over to Lexi. He pushed the phone back into her pocket. "Your mom is real nice," he grinned.

"You're relentless," she breathed and rolled her eyes.

"If you didn't have that neck brace and medics surrounding you, I might try to kiss you."

She pursed her lips to keep from smiling then averted her gaze.

∼

*A*fter a few x-rays, Lexi was cleared with no broken ribs and allowed to go home for the evening. Robert pushed her toward the automatic doors. "Well, my Pop rode to the rodeo with Sabrina and picked up the Dually. They drove it here and dropped it off. I have the keys." He shook them in his hands.

She looked up at him with raised brows. "And you plan on taking me home?"

"Not quite."

"Well, it's been an eventful evening and honestly, I'm tired. I'm not up for much else." She looked away and sighed, then wheezed from the pain. "I'm sorry."

"Sorry for what? Being in the wrong place at the wrong time?

Think nothing of it. I'm not taking you home yet because you're coming home with me."

"What?" She looked back to him with a questioning gaze.

"I'm taking you home with me. Pop and Sabrina have a tasting to do in Dallas tomorrow so they're staying the night there." He pushed her wheelchair outside toward the truck. "It's just us tonight."

"Robert," she started and her hands gripped the armrests of the wheelchair.

"What? I told you nothing is going to happen. I'm simply going to keep an eye on you. And to set your mind at rest, I got permission from your mother first. If you notice, she's not here."

Lexi seemed to realize this for the first time and looked around the parking lot as she stood up. "Where... where did she go?" She turned back to him and held onto her ribs.

"Home." He opened the door for her and assisted her into the big truck. He walked around to his side and climbed in. He started the truck then turned to her with her pain medicine. He was about to speak when she started.

"Robert, I can't do this." She said it so quickly she wondered if it sounded like one word.

"You can't take your pain medicine?" He knew exactly what she was saying, but tried to put her at ease anyway.

"Please," she started.

"Lexi, now you listen to me. Stop being such a stubborn woman! I'm trying to take care of you here, so let me. Stop fighting it and allow me to help. That's all I want to do."

"Help?" She shook her head. "You're doing more than helping me here and you know it." She looked away from him and tried to huff, but she winced in pain again.

"Are you ready to take something or will you continue to be a pain in my ass?"

She looked over to him with her mouth wide open. "How DARE you!"

He busted out laughing. "Yes, how dare I take care of you when I could have left you here? How dare I actually care to be here and take care of you? How dare I be concerned if you will be okay tonight? How dare I even consider a transfer of schools?"

"What?" She whispered.

"It doesn't matter. You obviously don't want me so I'll take you home." He put the truck into gear and felt his heart ripping in his chest.

Before he took off, Lexi took her seatbelt off and scooted across the seat. She moved over until their thighs pressed against one another. She rested her small, delicate hand on his strong, forearm. "I'm sorry," she whispered.

He looked over at her for a moment and watched her. He looked out the window and put the truck back into park. "Damn, you're a pain in my ass, Lexi."

"I'm sorry," she whispered again.

He looked back at her again then blinked. "Shit, don't cry." He wrapped his arm around her and pulled her close. "I'm sorry, baby, I didn't mean it."

She sobbed then winced. "Dammit, this really hurts."

"I know it does. Let me take you home and I'll..."

"No, take me to your place, please. I want to."

"Are you sure?" He looked down into her eyes.

"Yes, I'm positive." She looked up and wiped her tears. "I'm so sorry. You're not him. I know you're not. I just can't help..."

"I know, been there. It's okay. You're not ready and I respect that. Let's just go. We can talk about it in the morning, okay?"

She nodded and buried her face in his chest again. "Thank you," she whispered.

"There's nothing to thank me for, but you're welcome." He kissed the top of her head. "I would do anything for you," he whispered.

∾

*R*obert helped her into the house and turned on the lights. They took the stairs up and he led her into the bathroom. "I'll get a t-shirt of mine and some shorts. I'll be happy to help you shower, if you want?" He grinned at her and waggled his brows.

She smiled and tried not to laugh. "I'm good. Just the t-shirt and shorts please. But, you may need to help me get undressed."

"Oh, I can definitely help with that." He rubbed his hands together with excitement.

"Bobby Ray, seriously, please?"

He chuckled. "Of course, I'll be a perfect gentleman. Let me... umm..." He watched her for a moment then held up a hand. "I'll be right back." He turned and ran out of the room.

She shook her head and looked in the bathroom mirror. She blinked looking at herself. "Oh damn, I look like hell! Maybe a shower wouldn't be a bad idea."

"You want to shower?" He asked standing in the doorway. She looked down and found him holding a white t-shirt and a pair of boxers.

"Umm, maybe not. But I'd like to wash my face, if I could?"

"You bet." He set the clothes down and reached for a wash cloth. "Wash your face and I'll help you in here, okay?" She nodded and he turned, closing the door behind him, giving her some privacy. He thought about that for a moment, knowing he was about to see her pretty much naked and he chuckled.

A moment later, the door opened and she walked out. He looked over at her and raised his brows. "You washed your face?"

She nodded and looked up. "I did."

"Wow, you're even more beautiful, if that were possible."

She smiled. "Thank you."

"You're welcome. Now c'mere and let me get you naked."

Her eyes opened wide in shock.

"Woman, I'm kidding." He smiled and motioned for her to

come closer. He could see her hesitate for a moment then he relaxed as she crossed the room.

He gently touched her cheek and offered a smile. He looked down at her blouse and reached for it. He began to unbutton her top, exposing her breasts. He swallowed and looked into her eyes. She smiled and he grinned. He looked back down as he neared her stomach.

He gently pulled the shirt over her shoulders, then down her arms. She softly gasped.

"I'm sorry." He pressed his lips together. She nodded and he pulled it over her hands. Robert looked down her slender, beautiful body. Her breasts were perky and absolutely perfect. Her stomach was flat and had a soft line running down the middle. He imagined for a moment his tongue running up its length.

She cleared her throat and he looked into her eyes. "Sorry," he mumbled. She smiled and shook her head. She reached for her pants and unbuttoned them. He stepped closer and slid his fingers into her jeans. "I honestly thought about this moment much differently."

She laughed then caught her breath. "Please don't make me laugh!"

"I'm sorry! So sorry, baby, I really am."

She smiled and looked up at him. "I like it when you call me baby."

"I like calling you baby." He winked and began pushing her jeans down. He went over her backside and tried to keep his fingers from grasping her firm ass cheeks. But damn, did he want to grab them!

He kneeled in front of her and lifted her left leg out, then the right. He stood and took in the sight of Lexi in her black bra and panties. "Damn, woman, the good lord definitely blessed you."

She blushed with a smile and averted her gaze. "Thank you."

He touched her cheek and brought her face back up again.

"You're welcome." He leaned in and kissed her gently. He lingered on her lips for a moment then pulled away.

"I can't sleep in my bra," she whispered.

He glanced at her with a raised brow. "Umm... well?" He rested his hand over his mouth then tilted his head with raised brows while he stared at her breasts.

"Robert Shaw. Stop it." She smiled and turned around. "Unfasten my bra, please."

He grinned and reached for her. He hesitated for a moment before he gathered her hair at the nape of her neck. He shifted it to the side and allowed his eyes to take in her back. She had this birthmark over her left shoulder that looked like a strawberry.

Robert gently touched the top of her back, between her shoulders, and let his fingers gently move down her spine. She gasped softly and he watched the chills cover her back. He reached her bra and moved his fingers underneath it.

"Your fingers are cold." She smiled and looked over her shoulder at him.

He met her gaze and gave her a smirk. He unfastened her bra and watched as her back became entirely exposed to him. He wanted to kiss her spine, her shoulders, even the small of her back.

"Will you help me get the t-shirt on?" She asked.

She broke him from his thoughts and he sighed. "Yep." He picked up the t-shirt and helped pull it over her head. She fed in one arm and he held the shirt open for the other.

She turned back to face him and kept her eyes downcast. He tilted his head watching her. "You okay? I mean, other than the obvious?"

She nodded then looked up. "Yes."

He smiled and helped her into the shorts. He pulled down the comforter and sheets then helped her in. "Comfortable?"

"Not yet, but I will be." She smiled up at him and he raised his brow.

"Well, give me just a moment and I'll make sure you're mighty comfy." He winked. Robert untucked his shirt and began to unbutton it. He noticed she didn't look away... and he liked it.

He pulled off his shirt and exposed a white t-shirt underneath. He laid the button down across the chair in his room. He removed his boots and socks. He then unbuckled the belt, unbuttoned his pants and removed them. Standing in his t-shirt and boxers, he watched her for a moment and saw a look of satisfaction in her gaze.

He grinned and pulled his t-shirt over his head. He heard her gasp and when looked at her, he noticed she wasn't in pain. Matter of fact, he noticed the look of satisfaction had shifted into lust. He chuckled and grinned. "Settle down, woman."

"What? I didn't say anything."

"You didn't have to." He chuckled again. He stepped closer to the bed and climbed in, lying down.

"I had no idea you were so... damn, Robert."

He laughed and turned on his side. "Yeah you did. Cliff diving. Oh, wait, are the pain meds kicking in now? If you have no filter, this could be fun."

"Oh, I'll show you fun!" She leaned toward him and captured his lips.

He kissed her and as much as he'd love to push her on her back and kiss every inch of her body, he knew it would be wrong. "Lexi, let's talk in the morning. Your meds have kicked in and I won't do that."

"What, you don't want me?" She pouted at him.

"Oh, trust me, I want you. Very much so. Just not when you're under the influence." He kissed her forehead then laid her back. "Just relax and go to sleep. We can make out in the morning."

"Oh goodie!" She smiled and closed her eyes.

He watched her for a moment in the darkness. Her outline in his bed was like looking at an angel. Her hair was tousled in a way that made her look sexy. Her lips were slightly parted and her breathes became longer and more into rhythm. He knew she had fallen asleep.

He turned on his back and stared at his ceiling. "I finally get her in my bed... because she's hurt. Perfect." He shook his head and grinned, then turned on his side, allowing sleep to take him under.

CHAPTER 9

$\mathcal{T}$he next morning, Robert woke first and found himself almost face to face with Lexi. Her lips were barely apart as she breathed. Her eyes were peaceful and her hands were tucked underneath her pillow. She looked like an angel. He smiled and continued to watch her, then gently reached for her, pushing a strand of hair from her face.

She stirred slightly and when she inhaled, she snored softly. Robert tried not to chuckle. She stretched in the bed beside him then she groaned. He watched as she opened her eyes and looked at him, before she smiled.

"Good morning," he spoke.

She closed her eyes again, "Good morning, yourself." She snuggled closer to him and buried her face in his chest.

"Well this is not what I was expecting, but I like it."

"What?" She pulled back and looked at him, and this time, really looked. "Oh my god! Where am I?" She scooted across the bed and sat up quickly. "OW! What the hell?" She grabbed at her side in agony.

He sat up slowly and watched her face recall the events from the night before. "Lexi," he started. "You got kicked by a horse last night. You went to the hospital..."

She cut him off and looked over at him. "I remember all of that. I'm a little vague on how I ended up in your bed," she looked down at herself, "and in your clothes." She looked back up at him again and this time, the panic of being in his bed was slowly replaced by the sheer pleasure of her eyes drinking him in.

He sat there shirtless and in his boxers. He ran a hand through his messy hair and gave her a questioning look. "Well, after you were released, I told your mom I would be happy to take care of you."

"You did what?" She tore her eyes away from his chest and furrowed her brows. "Why would you do that?"

"Why wouldn't I have done it? Because I care about you," he told her. "Nothing happened, if you're so damn worried that it did." He lay back down on his pillow and turned on his side, away from her. "You're welcome to go if that's what you want. I won't hold you here." He sighed and stared at the wall. The evening he'd planned hadn't gone at all like he'd intended. First, she had been kicked, then she'd gotten high from the drugs, and damn if she hadn't been sexy as hell when he'd undressed her.

Suddenly, he felt her fingers touch his arm. The mattress moved under her when she repositioned herself next to him. "I'm so sorry, I didn't mean... I wasn't being ungrateful. Please, forgive me?"

He turned onto his back and looked up into her blue eyes. Her hair was a mess from sleeping but she looked absolutely beautiful. He could see himself waking up next to her many more times... many more mornings. "It's alright."

"No, no it's not. I'm really sorry. You didn't deserve that. I'm just... Hell, I don't know what I am."

"I know what you are."

"You do?" She gave him a curious gaze.

"Yeah, you're beautiful, you're confused, you're slightly injured, but I think part of it is your pride." He grinned which caused her to roll her eyes. "And I think you're scared."

She nodded and lowered her gaze. "You scare the hell out of me, Bobby Ray." She took a deep breath then raised her gaze to meet his.

"Not as much as you scare me," he told her. His ran his hand softly up her arm, then touched her cheek.

She leaned into his palm and closed her eyes. "How is it I could possibly scare you?"

"Because you have my heart… in your hands."

Her eyes opened wide with alarm. "What?"

He sighed, the nodded. "I can't help it. As much as I keep telling myself not to, I find myself wanting to be with you, always thinking about you, wondering what you're doing and hoping like hell you'll have me. These last few weeks, hell, this last month, has been one of the most amazing experiences of my life. You deserve so much more than you have. And you deserve to be happy. I want to make you happy, Lexi."

She blinked, but didn't say anything. Her mouth opened, then closed, then opened again. She tried to talk, but nothing came out. She turned her gaze across the room and her eyes landed on a picture of him when he was ten years old. In it was Conner, Makayla, Brad and a few others that had all graduated high school together. Everyone had a smile on their face and no one had any clue as to what lay ahead of them. Shortly thereafter, Robert moved away. A smile formed as she thought of the simpler times.

He watched her; curious as to what she was thinking. He sat up and adjusted himself so that he was closer to her. "Lexi, I'm not trying to put you in a position to…"

She turned to him with the same smile still on her lips. She shook her head and kept her eyes on his. "Shh, don't. It's okay." She moved closer to him on the bed then lay on her side. She put her arm under her head and reached over and traced the outline of his cheek, then looked into his eyes. "Robert, no one has ever said anything like that to me. Ever." Her voiced turned into a whisper. "I want you, too. So very much."

He watched her for a moment, his eyes searched hers for the truth... and he found it staring back at him. He ran his hand gently up her arm, then ran his fingertips across the line of her hair. "You're so beautiful," he breathed. He cupped her face, leaned in, and kissed her.

Her hands moved to his bare chest and they shook ever so slightly. He pulled back and looked into her eyes. "Lexi, it's okay. We don't have to..."

She shook her head and leaned into him. She kissed him and ran her hand around his neck and she pulled him closer. His arm moved around her waist then he slipped his hand up the inside of her t-shirt, moving over her back.

Her leg moved between his. She gently bit his bottom lip and tugged. He opened his eyes and watched her with a smirk. "You like to nibble?"

She giggled and kissed him again. Robert pushed her onto her back and rolled on top of her, making sure to keep his body weight off her. She gasped softly against his lips and he pulled away. "I'm okay, just sore from last night."

"Normally, that would inflate my ego, a woman telling me they're sore from last night." He smirked.

"Oh god, Bobby Ray!" She laughed then gasped again.

"Okay, well let me get downstairs and I'll start us breakfast. Sound good?" He moved off her with a groan. Keeping his back to her, he adjusted himself in his boxers, and stood.

She took note and found herself looking down. Her brows raised and her lips parted. He cleared his throat and she suddenly looked up, her face turning red. "Oh shit!" She hid her face in the pillows and Robert laughed out loud.

"It's fine, promise. I don't mind you admiring my shit. C'mon now, look!"

"No! Not if you're going to whip it out and twirl it!"

He laughed even harder. "Hardly. I'll save that for later."

"Please tell me you're kidding!" She finally looked up and found him across the room.

Robert reached for the stereo and turned it on. He flipped through the stations and landed on *You Can Leave Your Hat On* by Joe Cocker. He grinned and looked back at Lexi. He found her smiling with a raised brow.

He moved across the room and shook his ass enough to make it seductive, yet funny. He walked to the doorframe and grabbed it then started moving against it seductively. He dipped down and swayed his ass side to side. He came up and pretended to run his tongue up the length of the frame.

Lexi covered her face and giggled uncontrollably into her hands. Her side shot in pain but for the moment, she ignored it. She shook her head then yelled out, "TAKE IT OFF!"

He laughed and shook a finger at her. He danced around the room a little more then pushed his boxers down enough to show his ass cheeks. She squealed and he pulled them back up. Robert moved to the other side of the door, disappearing behind it. He peeked back into the room and waggled his brows, before he came back into the room. He gyrated his hips and his arms moved in rhythm above his head

As the song faded out, he made his way back over to the bed to his girl… who was now crying, she was laughing so hard. "Oh my god, my side hurts!"

"Damn baby, I hope you're not laughing at my mad skills." He chuckled and kissed her cheek.

"No…" she laughed, trying to get control of herself, "no one has ever…," she laughed some more, "ever done that for me! DO IT AGAIN!"

He shook his head with a smile. "Maybe after breakfast, baby." He winked with a smile the headed toward the door. "Meet me downstairs once you're done laughing."

Grinning, Robert headed downstairs and opened the fridge. He pulled out eggs, bacon, and butter. Setting everything up, he turned on the television and listened to the news while he started on the bacon. He started up the coffee then reached for the sun tea container and filled it with water. Setting the tea bags inside, he opened the kitchen door and set it on the porch. Closing the screen door, he let in fresh air then made his way back to the bacon.

He leaned against the island in the kitchen and looked around while singing *You Can Keep Your Hat On* to himself.

The kitchen itself hadn't changed much since he'd last seen it. The walls were still the same tan color Sabrina painted it all those years ago. The dining room table was smaller and somewhat new. His father had replaced the countertops with granite sometime back. The light color made the kitchen look brighter.

"Smells good in here."

He turned and found Lexi coming down the stairs in the same t-shirt and boxers; he noticed she had put on her bra.

"It'll be ready in a bit. Get comfy. Coffee's on if you'd like some, or there's coke in the fridge. I put out sun tea a few minutes ago."

"I'll have some coffee, thanks." She leaned against the counter next to him and leaned her head on his shoulder.

He wrapped his arm around her then kissed the top of her head. "Good morning."

She smiled. "Yes it is, if you wake me with a dance like that every morning." She looked up with a teasing glance.

"Yeah, right. Not happening."

"Oh man! To think, I was so hopeful!" She grinned and wrapped her arms around his solid waist.

"I need to turn the bacon." He looked down at her with a smile. "But I'm going to kiss you first." He tilted up her chin, smiled, and kissed her. He opened her mouth with his tongue and held her captive for a few minutes.

A few cups of coffee and a breakfast later, they finished up and decided it was as good a time as any to head back into town.

"I should call my mom; let her know I'm okay." She stood up from the table, but not before Robert pulled her back onto his lap.

"Tell her how good I took care of you, but feel free to leave the part with the dancing out. You don't need to scar her like that."

She shook her head. "My side hurt so much from all that laughing, Bobby Ray. You owe me big!"

"Well, then I intend to absolutely pay it up."

∼

*A*bby pulled down the street Lexi lived on and parked in front of her house. She saw her car in the driveway and decided to go pay her friend a visit. She stepped up to the front door, straightened her shirt, and knocked.

A moment later, Lexi's mother answered the door. "Hey Abby, what brings you by?"

"Morning, Mrs. Griffin. I came by to see Lexi. Is she here?" She smiled at the older woman.

"No, I'm afraid not."

Abby's brows rose in surprise. "She's not here? Mrs. Griffin, it's early, did she run into town? Maybe I can catch her?"

"Oh no, dear, she's with her friend, Bobby Ray." Lexi's mother stepped outside and closed the door behind her. She motioned to the swing on the porch and took a seat, patting the spot next to her. Abby smiled and took a seat. Mrs. Griffin went into the details of the rodeo, the accident with the horse and Bobby Ray taking care of her.

"Oh... I see." Abby looked down and twisted her hands in her lap.

"What is it dear? What's wrong? Is it that boy?" Concern shot up on Mrs. Griffin's face and voice.

"No, not exactly." Abby looked at the woman and shrugged, as if asking for forgiveness in not knowing. "How well does she really know Bobby Ray? Besides that, what about Blaine? He would be so upset if he found out Lexi was cheating on him."

"Blaine would be upset?" Mrs. Griffin laughed. "Hardly. That boy has cheated on my Lexi every chance he's had. He'd do the world a huge favor if his pecker fell off. He broke my baby's heart. Besides, why do you care so much about what happens to Blaine?" The woman gave her a cold look.

Abby shook her head and raised her hands in surrender. "He's my friend, too, that's all I'm saying. I thought they were still together. I didn't realize they had broken up." She was lying and she knew it. Blaine was coming back to town and the more ammo she had, the more she could hurt Lexi with it. *How dare she cheat on Blaine,* she told herself.

"Your friend or not, honestly Abby, I thought better of you. You may want to consider different friends." Mrs. Griffin stood and headed toward the front door. She looked over her shoulder to the girl. "I'll tell Lexi you came by." With that, she went inside and closed the door.

Abby stood and shook her head, then headed off the colonial style porch. She walked down to her car and got inside. After starting it up and turning the a/c on, she pulled out her phone and brought up Blaine's text. She hit reply.

When are you coming into town? Lexi is fucking Bobby Ray probably right about now. Her mama even thinks your pecker should fall off. Her words, not mine. You need to get back here and make it quick. I miss you.

She pressed send and dropped her phone inside her purse. She was determined to get Blaine back here for her, not for Lexi. She wanted them apart for good and the only way to do that was to have Lexi or Bobby Ray catch them in the act. She smirked, put her car into gear. and drove off.

CHAPTER 10

$\mathcal{T}$he county fair set up and opened for business a few days later. Lexi had the day off and Robert picked her up that morning. She walked out of her house in mid-thigh denim shorts, bright tank top, and tan wedge sandals. Her hair was pulled into a pony tail with a pink ribbon tied around it. Her skin looked golden from lying out in the sun and Robert's eyes widened when he took in the sight of her.

He catcalled to her with a grin. "Damn woman, you're looking mighty fine today." He opened his arms for her and embraced her tightly. He turned his baseball cap backwards then leaned in to kiss her.

"You don't look too bad yourself." She grinned and kissed him back. She took in his baby blue t-shirt, khaki shorts, and University of Georgia baseball hat. Ray Bans covered his eyes and she could see her reflection in the lenses. "I swear to you, you'll be called out soon enough for wearing that hat around here."

Robert moved his hands to her butt and squeezed it. She giggled. "Yeah right. Ready to head out?"

"You bet."

He released her then opened the door to the Dually and she

climbed inside. He smacked her butt and she laughed as he shut the door.

He walked to the other side and climbed in, then turned on the radio. *Toby Keith* played through the speakers and he took off down the road. "Is there anything you won't ride or do at the fair? So I'll know ahead of time to steer clear of that area?"

"You'd do that for me?" She asked with a smile.

"Of course. I wouldn't make you do something that scared the crap out of you. That and are you still sore from the other night?"

She snorted and shook her head. "I'm pretty much healed up; however, that takes you out of the equation." She gave him a playful glare.

He groaned. "You're killing me!" He grinned at her. "Wow, I guess I walked into that one."

"One for Lexi, zero for Bobby Ray." She laughed. "Okay, so in all seriousness here... I guess the coasters. Ones at the actual amusement park don't bother me, but considering how often the ones at the fair are put up and taken down," she shook her head, "no thank you."

"Hell girl, I got you there. No coasters."

"What about you?" She asked him.

Robert turned down the path toward the fair and shook his head. "I think I'm pretty good on anything. Although, I get what you're saying and it's made me think about riding coasters in the future."

"Oh, I'm sorry," she told him.

"Nah, it's okay," he winked at her. A short while later, he pulled into the parking lot then they walked up to the ticket counter. He pulled out his wallet and waved her money away. "It's on me." He smiled and gave her a hug.

"Ahh, such a nice young man," said the woman behind the glass. She looked to be about sixty-five or so. Robert nodded to her and handed her forty dollars. She pushed the tickets through for them.

He took Lexi's hand and they walked into the fair, taking in the sights, the sounds of the games, and the smell of popcorn, turkey legs, and cotton candy.

"You hungry? You want anything?" He asked her.

"I'm thirsty. I could use some water."

He nodded, they walked to a vendor, and he bought them two bottles of cold water. They walked around a little more and she said hi to a few people she knew. They took in a few rides then ended up shooting the pellet gun riffles at mechanical ducks. "I swear these things are rigged!" He spouted off in anger at missing.

Lexi shot a few times and knocked a few down. "My gun is just fine. You just suck, mister." She giggled and sat the gun down. The manager offered her a stuffed animal. She cuddled it playfully, making kissy faces at it. Robert just smiled.

As the night ended and the fair began to shut down, they left and Robert followed the road back toward Lexi's home. "Do we have to go back yet?" She asked him.

"Well no, I suppose not." He glanced over at her. "Where would you like to go?"

"I don't know." She looked out her passenger window. "Maybe out to the lake to watch the stars?" She shifted her gaze back over to him.

Robert raised his brows at the gentle shyness she gave off. Was she suggesting something else to him? He surely didn't want to assume as much. "Sure, we can go there. Pop used to pack blankets and such in the tool box, just in case he needed to get under the truck."

"Afraid he'd get dirty?" She teased him.

"Well no, not exactly. He didn't want to lay in stickers or ant beds."

"Oh, well there IS that," she mused. She crossed her fingers in her lap and sighed.

Robert drove down the path to the lake and found a spot to park the truck. It had coverage of the trees, but not enough to block out the view of the night sky. There were no other cars around them so they at least had privacy.

He shut off the truck and cleared his throat. He glanced over at her and could see the nervousness in her face. "Lexi?"

"Yeah?" She looked over at him vulnerably.

"Nothing has to happen." He smiled at her.

She sighed and nodded. "I know." She opened her door and climbed out.

Robert followed suit and met her at the tailgate. He lowered it then jumped into the bed. He walked to the cab and opened the tool box. A minute later, he pulled out a red blanket and shook it out. He laid it across the bed of the truck then looked at Lexi. "Alright, here we go."

She bit her lip, and reached for Robert. He offered her a hand and pulled her onto the bed of the truck. She sat down on her knees, relaxed, and lay on her back. She looked up at Robert and found him watching her. "What?" She smiled.

He shook his head. "You look beautiful under the night sky." He tilted his head then ran his hand over his chin. "Hmm…"

"What are you doing?" She asked with a smile.

He then pretended to jump toward her, as if he were going to tackle her. She screamed and Robert laughed. He sat down next to her and grabbed her thigh, giving it a squeeze. "You're too easy sometimes."

"You're an ass!" She slapped his arm playfully. "Lay down here with me."

He did as she asked and laid back. She rolled onto her side and as he wrapped his arm underneath her neck, she laid her head on his chest. "This is nice," she said with a smile. "Oh, I hear your heart."

"Oh yeah? What's it saying?"

"Sounds like… must, thump, thump, get in, thump, thump, Lexi's panties, thump, thump." She giggled.

"Oh wow, you heard all that?" he chuckled.

"Sure did," she smiled and raised her head to look at him. She ran her fingers across his cheek gently.

He laid there watching her. Her beauty made him want to close his eyes, and hold onto this moment before it was gone. He would be leaving soon and he had a decision to make, change schools and be here with her, or go back and end this romance. He didn't want the latter so he felt there was only one thing he could do. "Lexi, I need to ask you something serious."

"Oh, okay." She sat up and folded her legs underneath her then rested her elbows on her knees. "I'm listening."

He sat up and folded his legs. He rubbed his forehead and thought about how to word what he wanted to say to her. "You know how I feel about you, right?" He glanced over at her.

"Yeah, I'm pretty sure I do." She smiled. "Why?" Her face grew troubled. "Is this about the end of summer?"

"Sort of," he said. "But before you go and get any ideas, I need you to hear me out." She nodded and her smile dropped into more of a frown. "There's a lot I thought I had to consider when we decided to go out. Honestly, I never expected all of what I feel for you to surface. And damn, if it didn't happen fast!" He shook his head.

Lexi lowered her gaze and nodded. "So you want to break it off with me?"

"What?" He asked. "No! I asked you to hear me out first. Damn, this isn't going like I thought it would."

She glared at him. "Well, then just say what you have to say and get it over with."

"Okay..." He furrowed his brows at her outburst and put himself in her shoes for a moment. *Hell, she thinks I am breaking up with her.* "What I'm trying to say is," he swallowed and scooted closer to her, then took her hand. "I want to be here with you."

"But you are here with me." She ran her thumb over his hand absently.

"No Lexi, I mean stay here, not go back to Georgia."

Her eyes widened at this. "What?" She asked.

He could see he'd caught her off guard and he sighed. "I know it's a lot to take in. I'm sorry to drop it on you like this, but I feel myself falling for you and damn if I can't stop it from happening." He looked back into her eyes again. "And at this point, I don't want to stop it."

"You don't?" She whispered. Her bottom lip trembled slightly and her eyes began to water.

He shook his head. "No, I don't. I've made a few calls to the University here. The transfer would be easy. I just show up for classes and…" He stops when she suddenly threw herself at him in a hug.

"I can't believe you'd do that for me!" She sobbed softly in his ear and her arms tightened around his neck.

"I can't imagine going back without you." His arms tightened around her back. "I want to love you, if you'll let me."

She pulled back and wiped underneath her eyes. She smiled and hiccupped. "Of course, I'll let you!" She cupped his face and kissed him.

Robert pulled away just enough to rest his forehead against hers. He asked, "So, will you be my girl?"

She grinned, "As long as I can call you my man."

"You got yourself a deal." He winked then kissed her again, but this time, with more passion. His tongue slid across her lips and she opened her mouth. He found her tongue and his hands moved into her hair, holding her close.

Robert leaned into her and laid her on her back. Lexi's arms reached up wrapped around his neck. He pushed his leg in between hers and rested on top of her, keeping his weight on his arms.

He trailed his lips to her neck and kissed her just underneath her ear. He felt her shiver and he grinned against her neck. He lifted up just enough to look in her eyes. He didn't miss the longing in her eyes.

Lexi tugged at his neck and pulled him back down to her. They kissed again and she moved her outer leg up against his, causing her hips to grind against him.

He groaned into her lips and moved against her. She gasped and her fingers moved into his hair, giving it a tug. Robert moved his free hand to her breast and he squeezed it, feeling her taut nipple against his palm. He kissed down her neck again and gently tugged her shirt down.

Exposing her breast through her thin bra, Robert licked at her nipple and she gasped again. Her hands pulled him closer to her breasts and he took advantage of it. His fingers pulled the bra down over her nipple and he suckled the mound between his lips.

She moved her body against his and a soft whimper left her lips. He glanced up at her then ran his hand under her back to her bra. He unfastened it then moved her shirt up, over her head. He looked down at her body and found the bruise from the horse beginning to fade. He then pulled her bra off her body and set it aside.

"Is this okay?" He asked her before he continued.

She nodded and tugged at his shirt. "Take it off. I want to feel you against me." He reached over his head to grab at the material. He pulled it off, and tossed it. He leaned back against her and kissed her hard. His body moved against her and his erection pressed against his shorts.

Her legs moved on either side of him and she wrapped them around his waist. Robert's chest moved against hers, the feeling of her breasts bare against his body made his erection that much harder. "Fuck, I want you," he whispered.

"Then take me," she told him and bit his lip.

He gave her a look filled with lust and he growled. "Oh, I plan on it."

She gasped, watching him when he sat up. Robert unbuttoned her shorts and pulled them down her body, leaving her in her lacy panties. "Godammit, those are fucking sexy!"

She smiled and bit her lip. "I like wearing sexy lingerie. Well, especially now with you here. I wasn't sure if I'd ever get to show them to you."

"What?" He asked, almost shocked. "You've been waiting for me to make this move?" He smirked and reached for her, moving a finger down the lining of her panties. "Damn, you're wet."

"You turn me on, baby. And yeah, I've been waiting for this." She grinned and her breath came out in a shudder. Butterflies flew through her stomach and she raised her brow. "Well, are you going to finish getting me naked?"

He raised his brows with surprise. "Damn, woman!" He chuckled and she laughed. He hooked his fingers to either side of her panties and tugged them down her legs. She lifted her hips to help him.

He set them down next to her clothes and took in the sight of Lexi Griffin. "You have to be the most beautiful, most enticing, most sexy... is that a word? Most sexy?"

She giggled and shrugged. "I guess it is now."

"Alright, most fucking sexy woman I've ever met." Her legs were bent and he ran his hands over her smooth skin, down to her hips. He moved between her legs and pushed them apart. He kissed down her thighs and occasionally, looked up at her.

She bit her lips again watching him. Her hands moved into his hair and occasionally she would jump if he found a ticklish spot. He made a mental note to remember that for later.

As he drew closer, he kissed over her sex and she gasped. He glanced up to her and found her eyes closed, enjoying him. He slid his arms underneath her hips then gripping her thighs, he pulled himself against her folds.

She gasped louder and her hands moved into his hair, pulling him harder against her. He remained there on her for a bit, tasting her while she moaned. Her hips bucked against him when he would find a sensitive spot.

Robert withdrew his tongue from her then slowly, moved up

her body. He kissed up her stomach to her breasts. He sucked her nipples for a few minutes then finally sat up. He looked down on her naked body with a grin. "Good lord, baby, you're beautiful."

"Take off your pants, baby. Come down here to me." She grinned. "Oh, do you have protection?"

He nodded and pulled it from his pants pocket then showed her.

"You always have one with you?" She asked with raised curiosity.

"Well no, not always. Just after the morning we woke up in bed together. After that morning, I started carrying it, just in case." He winked and set it on her stomach. "Now, don't you move." He grinned, then unbuttoned his pants and pushed them down with his boxers. He kicked them off to the side.

She looked down and took in the sight of his dick. Her eyes widened then looked back at him.

"Are you okay?" He asked her.

"Uh huh," she said and swallowed. "I just didn't realize you were... well... so endowed."

He chuckled. "Don't let it scare you. I won't be rough, I mean, unless you're into that kind of thing."

"I might be... but not yet." She looked down again, then back up.

He grinned, "You might be? Well, I might be open to tying your sexy ass up." He opened the condom and rolled it on. He tossed the packaging then looked at her. He leaned over her body and looked into her eyes. "It's okay if you're not ready. We don't have to..."

Suddenly, Lexi grabbed his neck and pulled him down, kissing him. He took it she was ready and reached down between them, grabbing his dick. He pressed it against her and entered her.

She gasped as he glided inside, hitting her base. "Oh god," she moaned.

He pulled back and gently pushed back inside. "Does it hurt?"

"Oh god, no, keep going," she whispered. Her hands moved from his neck to his biceps. She squeezed as he thrust inside her again. "Robert..." She moaned his name and her head rolled back. He leaned in and kissed her neck. He began to thrust a little harder, still keeping a slow pace. Their bodies moved together as one and he fit perfectly inside her. She moaned a little louder and her back arched.

Robert pulled back and thrust hard into her and she yelled out. "Did I hurt you?" He asked with concern.

She shook her head. "No, do it again," she whispered. She looked into his eyes then raised her head and kissed him.

He did as she asked and thrust harder, moving a little faster. She moaned louder and rested her head against the bed of the truck.

Her back arched against him again. "Oh my god, don't stop," she begged him. "Oh my god!"

"Mmm, you like that, baby?" He asked and nibbled on her neck. "Damn, you feel so good Lexi!"

"Oh god, yes!" She moved her arms underneath his and held onto him.

Robert sat up on his heels then grabbed Lexi's hips, pulling her up to him. He held her while he thrust deep inside her core. He could feel himself building a release and knew he would need to slow down to make this last.

She grabbed at his arms and pulled herself up. Robert sat back as Lexi positioned herself on top of him. She moved her hips forward and back and her head tilted back toward the moon.

Robert moved his hands up her back and into her hair. He cupped the back of her head then kissed across her neck.

"I'm going to come," she whispered to him. Looking down into his eyes, she claimed his lips, and rode him harder.

Robert groaned against her lips as he spilled his seed inside the condom. "Fuck woman, come for me." He gripped her hair and pulled, exposing her neck. He kissed along the contours of it as she gasped. Lexi moaned into the air and gripped Robert's shoulders. "Oh, shit!"

Her body quivered for a moment as she rode the orgasm out.

The two lay together on the bed of the truck in each other's arms until the breeze was too much on their naked bodies.

CHAPTER 11

*I*t was the middle of July and the weekend of Jim and Sabrina's wedding. Robert pulled on his tuxedo and looped the tie around his neck. He looked at his father in the mirror and found him fussing with his own tie. "Here Pop, allow me." Robert walked over and began to fix the tie.

"Thank you, son." Jim ran his hands down his thighs. "Hell, I'm nervous and the woman has lived with me for years... quite a few years. How can I be this nervous?"

Robert laid his hands on his father's shoulders. "She's not Mom. She's not going to leave you."

"Son, I know that." He smiled.

"I know, but sometimes you need to hear it... Even if it's been... what... almost twenty years?"

He nodded. "Sounds about right. When did you get all wise?"

"Ahh, hell, I don't know. Came with age, I suppose." Robert grinned.

"Right," Jim chuckled.

In the next room, Sabrina was a cool as a snowman. "I'm fine, y'all! Stop making such a damn fuss! My dress isn't white because y'all should know it's no secret. Jim and I have sex."

The ladies in the room laughed and sipped on more champagne. A light rap knocked on the door and Lexi peeked inside. "May I come in?"

"Oh honey, come on in!" Sabrina stood and her black dress flowed around her.

Lexi gasped and took in the beautiful dress. Black satin and sleeveless, the dress fit Sabrina perfectly. The waist was tight and the skirt flowed out like a princess dress. "Sabrina, you look like you're marrying Prince Charming."

"Well, honey, I am!" She winked. "My god darling, you look absolutely stunning yourself! Has Bobby Ray seen you yet?" Sabrina shook her head with a smile. "I reckon if he did he wouldn't let you leave his sight looking the way you do."

Lexi blushed pink. It almost matched her dress. "Thank you, but no, he's not seen me yet. I'm giving him the element of surprise!" She grinned.

"Well, this will definitely do that for you. Hmm, I suggest staying hidden from him until the wedding is about to begin, then have an usher bring you in while Bobby Ray and Jim are waiting for me and my gals to come down the aisle."

"Oh, that's a perfect idea!" Lexi giggled. "You sure you don't mind?"

"Mind? Hell, child I'll be waiting for my bitches in waiting to go first!" She bellowed out a laugh while her bridesmaids called her questionable names.

Lexi wondered if Sabrina already had too much champagne.

"It's almost time, ladies!" The call came in from the other side of the door.

"That sounded like the minister's wife," Sabrina told Lexi. "Well, it's time! Shit, do I look okay?" She began fussing over her dress and looked in the mirror. "Oh god, why did I decide on black? I'm getting married, not dying! Why did y'all let me get this blasted thing?"

Lexi's brows rose. The bridesmaids crossed the room and

began consoling her, telling her that they didn't believe in tradition.

Sabrina began to calm down and looked to Lexi. "Go on, we'll be out shortly."

Lexi nodded. "Give'em hell." She grinned at her boyfriend's soon to be step-mom. She opened the door, stepped out, and closed it behind her.

She made her way toward the garden area where the wedding was set up. A beautiful archway with fresh white roses stood at the beginning of the walk and a black carpet led the way to the altar.

She nodded and smiled at an usher as Jim and Robert made their way to their positions. She caught Robert's gaze and Sabrina was right, she was giving him an eye full.

Robert took her in... all of her. The dress she had hidden underneath the black one... this must be the one. He shook his head with a smile. The light pink silky fabric clung to her body. The one shoulder sleeve left one arm bare. The bottom of the dress clung to her thighs... her mid-thigh. He wondered for a moment if she were wearing panties as there's no way this dress could hide any kind of panty line.

He swallowed hard and tried to adjust the growing erection in his pants. "Good god... damn, she looks good."

"Wipe your mouth, son." Jim chuckled.

The bridesmaids made their way down the aisle and stood in position. The music changed to the wedding march. Robert glanced at his father and found a smile... a true happiness smile, covering his lips.

Sabrina made her way down the aisle toward Jim by herself. She had informed Robert no one would be giving her away since she had no family left. The memory of that day made him smile at his future stepmother.

"Well you'll have us then as your family," he told her. She pulled him a hug and told him she loved him as if he were her own son.

~

*W*hen the wedding ended, Robert walked down the aisle with a bridesmaid, his eyes on Lexi the entire time. As soon as the wedding was over, it was picture time.

Lexi sat in a picnic chair, legs crossed, sipping champagne. Occasionally, Robert looked over at her with a smile. Sometimes, it looked as if his eyes might pop out of his head and he'd pant like a dog, like the cartoon characters she used to watch when she was a child.

When the wedding pictures ended, Robert made his way over to Lexi and took a seat next to her. He leaned in and kissed her, slipping his tongue across her lips. She whimpered softly against his lips and he grinned. He pulled back just enough to look into her eyes. "Damn baby, you look so amazing!" His fingers gently glided over her cheeks. "C'mere, I'm kissing you again."

She giggled and leaned into him. *Click.* She looked up just as the photographer snapped a picture. "Well if you're taking our pictures, at least get my good side." She said and grinned, stood up, and sat on Robert's lap.

His hands moved around her waist and he held her close. He ran his fingers over her hips and gently across her ass. "You're not wearing panties, are you?" He whispered.

"Maybe, maybe not," she replied with a smile and the photographer snapped a few more pictures. When the photographer thanked them and went on to others to photograph, she turned to face him, still in his lap. "They're called *SPANX*, honey. And they're amazing."

He grinned then chuckled. "So... you're wearing granny panties. Hot."

She rolled her eyes. "Is that how you see me when I don't wear panties and wear my *SPANX* instead?"

"What? You're NOT wearing panties? Shit, that IS hot!"

"Wow, you're such a guy! There's no getting through to you, is there?" She smiled.

He pulled her close and whispered, "I think with my head. And when I say head, I mean my dick. I'm a guy," he shrugged. "It's what I do."

She shook her head. "You should be ashamed of yourself Bobby Ray!" She tried not to grin and failed miserably.

"Ashamed of myself? For what? Finding you sexy? Then by all means, please baby, hold it against me!" He laughed and kissed her again.

Robert stood up with Lexi and he pulled her toward the dance floor. "Come on, I want to dance with you." The song *Me and You* by Kenny Chesney began to play. Robert pulled her close and wrapped an arm around her waist.

Lexi placed her hand in his, the other around his neck. She leaned into him and stared into his eyes as a smile pulled her lips.

He led her around the dance floor and never broke eye contact. "I want to leave and take you with me. I need to get you out of this incredible dress and have my way with you." Robert leaned in and kissed her soft and slow. Not realizing they had stopped dancing. Someone said, "Excuse me," while another voice yelled out, "Get a room!" Robert chuckled and looked into Lexi's eyes. "Are you ready to go? Since we have a crowd?" He grinned.

She bit her lip for a moment and smiled. "Do you think we can stay long enough for the bouquet toss?"

"Sure, I don't see why not." He leaned in and kissed her neck, under her ear, then whispered, "Your loss if we don't leave now." He nibbled her ear and she swooned softly.

"Bobby Ray, people are watching."

"They're jealous," he told her with a chuckle.

A while later, they were in his truck and headed toward his house. His parents would be gone for the weekend and Robert planned to take advantage of the alone time with Lexi.

He glanced over at her while she played with the flowers on

the bouquet. He noticed the smile on her face. "What's on your mind? You look like you're up to something."

"Who me?" She looked over slowly, teasing him with her eyes. "I have no idea what you mean."

He grinned and turned back to the road. "Sure you don't."

Lexi set the flowers down and crossed her legs. "Do you believe in tradition that whoever catches the bouquet is the next to get married?" She glanced over to him for his reaction.

Robert shrugged and turned down his road. "I haven't ever given it a whole lot of thought before. I can honestly say I've never caught a bouquet." He looked over at her with a grin.

She smiled and nodded. "Well, I'd hope not. Because that would be... weird." She looked out the window then sighed. She turned back to Robert when she felt his hand take hers.

"You alright?"

"Yes, wonderful in fact. It's just... well? Your dad's wedding just happened. Next, you're moving here for me. I'm not sure I'm ready for that."

"Lexi," he started. He released her hand and turned down the long driveway toward his house. Dirt kicked up behind the Dually as he sped down the narrow drive.

Once he parked, he turned off the ignition and turned to her. "I didn't want to talk about this tonight. I was hoping to spend the weekend with you and not worry about anything."

"I know," she looked down and sighed. "I didn't mean to spoil anything." She looked back up. "Things between us have happened so fast and before I knew it, here we are. I just wasn't expecting this... hell, I wasn't expecting you, Robert."

There she was with his name again. He nodded then reached for her, touching her cheek. "Come on inside. Let's get a drink and sit down. We can discuss this inside and see where we end up."

"Alright." She leaned in and kissed him gently on his lips. "I'm sorry to be a party pooper."

"Oh baby, you didn't ruin anything. I still intend to get you naked. It's just a matter of getting you in the house."

She couldn't help herself. Lexi began to laugh. She sat back in her seat and laughed harder and harder until she wiped her tears.

He smiled watching her and reached over, combing her hair behind her ear. "You're so beautiful when you laugh."

"Thank you," she said in between giggles. "I'm sorry; I'm not laughing at you or anything like that. It's just… we got so serious for a moment and you still can't think of anything but me being naked!" She laughed again, this time with a snort.

This made Robert laugh. He shook his head. "You're a damn sexy woman, Lexi." He grabbed his keys and got out of the truck. He walked to her side and opened the door. His eyes took in her long, slender legs up to the beautiful mounds spilling over the top of her dress. He couldn't wait to see them and hold her naked body against his. He then looked into her eyes and found her smiling. "What?" He held her arms out for her.

She slid from the truck into his arms easily. "Oh nothing, other than you eye fucking me."

Robert chuckled. "Well, I want to do more than eye fuck you. Get inside woman!" He closed her door then, as she side stepped closer to him, he spanked her ass. She squealed and he chased her toward the door.

After making their way inside and turning on a few lights, Robert grabbed a couple of cold bottles of water from the fridge and handed her one. He took a drink then walked toward her. His fingers moved over her forehead lightly, then down her cheek to her shoulder. His eyes searched hers for a moment, before he smiled. "I think you can see right into my soul."

"I wish I could," she told him. "I want to know what it would say to me." She stepped closer and rested her palms on his chest.

"That you own it." He kissed her softly. "And to be careful with it." He kissed her again and slipped his tongue across the seam her lips, opening her mouth. Her fingers curled against his shirt and she sighed against his lips. When they parted, he asked her, "What would your soul say to me?"

"It's fragile and only recently healed by this amazing guy. She's ready to move forward with him." She pushed her arms around his neck and pulled him down to her. She captured his lips and kissed him a little harder, with need, and maybe a little desperation.

He made a sound between a sigh and a growl. His hands moved to her back and he pulled her even closer. His fingers dug into her skin and their kissing turned heavier. "Upstairs," he mumbled against her lips. "Now."

"Make me," she told him, then bit his lip.

"Ow! What the hell?" He pulled back and looked at the smirk on her lips.

"Oh, did that hurt?" She snickered then backed away from him playfully. "I guess you need to come find me, Bobby Ray!" She put emphasis on his nickname then giggled.

"Oh, you're so paying for that, woman!" he grinned and began to stalk her.

She squealed and turned to run up the stairs, laughing the entire time. He caught up to her at the top and scooped her up in his arms. "I'm never letting you go, you got that?"

Lexi wrapped her arms around his neck then kissed his cheek. "Never."

He walked them into his bedroom and kicked the door shut behind them.

CHAPTER 12

$\mathcal{L}$ast night's night show exploded when Deep Ember took to the stage. "The small town band from Fort Worth, Texas is here to rock your world!" The fans screamed and yelled, women pulled off their tops and threw bras at the stage. Blaine had started a reputation for himself as a love'em and leave'em kind of guy. No strings attached; just like he liked it.

He didn't usually see the same woman twice. "That shit would mean a relationship to a bitch. I'm not about no damn relationships," he'd told his band mates.

Well, that is except for Lexi Griffin. Deep down, he knew he'd loved her at one time, but not enough to remain faithful. Being in a relationship was no way to live a life while on the road, women basically sucking your dick at any turn and throwing themselves at you. Damn... had they thrown themselves.

"I go into my room after a set and women are lined up to suck my cock," he'd told them jokingly. At first, the band looked down on Blaine when he'd emerge with a woman... sometimes two, from his hotel room. He'd all but shove them out when he was done with them.

Since his text chat with Abby, he knew he needed to get back to

Fort Worth after their show in Abilene. He had a few days off and that was plenty of time for him to get back and smooth things out.

"Why do you string her along like that, man? She deserves better. Let her go," Matt, his drummer, had told him. "Stop fucking around if she doesn't mean anything to you."

"You need to mind your own fucking business." Blaine had turned away from him and taken the keys from one of the roadies. "Give me a day or two. I'll be back in time for our trip." He turned to George, the owner of the keys he'd taken. "I'll have her back all clean and shit. No worries."

"Not you I'm worried about. You need to be back in time or we leave, with or without you." George sat in a chair and raised a brow. "You can be replaced if you're late. Remember that, kid."

"Yeah, yeah. I'll be back." He chuckled then walked out the door. "He can't replace me," he mumbled under his breath. "I'm the damn face and voice of this band. They'd fail without me."

He pulled out his cell and sent a message to Abby.

I'm on my way. Get her ready for me.

He pressed send then put the car into drive, taking off for Fort Worth.

~

*L*exi hummed to herself while working in the back of the tack store, doing inventory. She smiled and danced around to Toby Keith on the radio. *"How do you like me now!"* She giggled and checked off a box on the form. The wedding the other night had gone off without a hitch. She spent the night making love to Robert and found it funny she walked a bit bow-legged. She was in love with him, totally and completely.

"Lexi?"

Pulled from her thoughts, she turned around to the sound of Abby's voice. She smiled and walked up to her friend and gave her a hug. "Hey girl! What'cha up to?"

Abby hugged her friend and rolled her eyes with a sigh. When Lexi pulled back, she put a smile on her lips. "Oh, nothing really. Hey," she stood back and crossed her arms over her chest. "Did you hear Deep Ember is back in Texas?"

Lexi's smile dropped. She shook her head. "No, I didn't know that." She turned away from Abby and went back to counting inventory. "How did you find out?"

She laughed and leaned against the wall. "There's this little thing called the internet? Their fan page has like, exploded!" She stepped farther into the tack room and stood next to Lexi. Abby placed a hand on her shoulder and turned Lexi to face her. "I think they're coming here to Fort Worth. Don't you want to see Blaine?"

"Not particularly." She hung her head then sighed. "He hurt me really badly, Abby." She looked back up at her friend. "You know this. Why would I want to see him?" She turned back toward the inventory. "I hope his dick shrivels up and falls off. He probably picked up some damn VD and gives it to anyone who gets on their knees for him." She smirked at the thought.

"Lexi! Don't say such things!" Abby spouted. "Well, I'm throwing a big party. You're invited and they'll probably be there." Lexi turned to face her again with wide eyes. Abby held her hands up. "Before you get all high and mighty on me, they're my friends, too, remember? They left a lot of people here, not just you. You would do well to remember that."

She raised a brow and huffed. "Excuse me?"

"You heard me." She crossed her arms over her chest again. "Let it go. He left you. You have Bobby Ray now, don't you? So why is it a problem?"

"I did let it go. I just wasn't expecting to see him, I guess." She shook her head. "I don't know if we'll go, Abby. Please understand…"

She cut her off. "No, you WILL be there. No excuses. Don't let him run your life for you. You need to face him at some point. You might as well do it with that hot piece of ass standing next to you."

Lexi's eyes widened. "Abby!" She shook her head. "I hate to admit it, but you're right. I need to face the music at some point. Oh, no pun intended." She set her clipboard down and sighed. "Back when my daddy died, it was hard for mama… hell, for me, too… to go into his closet, into his maintenance building out back… anything that was his. It was so hard, but at some point, we knew we had to. We did it together and held each other while we cried."

"Oh Lexi," She softened her voice and pulled Lexi into a hug. "I'm so sorry about your daddy. He'd be so proud of you right now." She pulled away and smiled. "Well, I mean you did drop out of college to work here, but he'd still be proud."

Lexi furrowed her brows. *Fucking bitch*, she thought to herself. "Look, I have to work to do; I'll call you later." She grabbed her clipboard and turned her back on Abby.

Giving her an incredulous look, Abby smirked. "Okay honey, talk to you then." She turned and walked out of the tack room and back out onto the sales floor. The manager, Joe, saw her coming through and waved to her. She waved back and gave him a wink. The old man grinned and shook his head. She heard him mumble something but ignored him.

Getting into her car, she pulled out her phone.

Match set. Show up, she'll be there. I can't wait to feel you inside me again!

She pressed send with a smirk. She set her phone down for a moment. It chimed and she pulled up a text from Blaine.

You're a goddamn goddess.

She grinned then replied.

You have no idea.

～

*R*obert sat back on the couch and watched Sabrina walk through the den. She stopped and looked back at him for a moment. "You look like sunshine just lit up your world, honey." She smiled at him. "Did you get yourself some sunshine?"

"Oh god, I'm not having this conversation with you." Robert laughed and got up off the couch. He walked into the kitchen, opened the fridge, and pulled out a Dr. Pepper. He popped the top and took a drink. He turned and found that Sabrina had followed him. She had this smirk on her face that clearly said *I know what you did!*

"Damn woman, I'm not talking about what I did or did not do with Lexi!" He shook his head and took another drink.

"Well, you don't have to. Your modesty, the blush on your face, and the way you're avoiding me tells me everything I need to know." She stepped closer. "Now you listen to me, Robert." Sabrina used his real name, not his nickname. He knew this was serious. She poked him in the chest. "You may just be here for the summer, but taking a girls heart, well that can last a lifetime. You really need to think about that."

He grinned and stood there watching her, not saying anything. She tilted her head and raised her brows. "Well, what the hell is that look for? What did I obviously miss?" She asked him.

"Oh, it's nothing," he told her with a chuckle. "I might be talking to the Dean of Admissions at TCU or UTA come Monday about transferring."

"What?!" She squealed then hugged her stepson. "Does she know?"

"Not yet, but we've talked a little about it." He sighed. "Now I have to tell my mother." His voice dropped an octave. "That won't be a fun conversation."

"Why? What could she say?" Sabrina asked.

"Don't throw your life away over a poor country girl the way I did for your father."

He could see he'd hit a sour spot when he heard Sabrina grit her teeth. "Well, obviously she knows best, doesn't she?" Sabrina turned and walked to the other side of the kitchen. She looked back at Robert. "You make up your own mind. We need lawyers and politicians here just as much as Georgia does. If she refuses to pay for your education..."

He stopped her. "She's not paying for it."

"What?" She turned to face him. "If you don't mind me asking, who is?"

"Rick has been paying for it. Since he's the senator of Georgia, it pretty much gets me into any college in Georgia I want. Probably any college period."

"Oh, right. Well there is that." She walked back toward Robert. "Maybe consider talking to him first? We like him, honey. He's a good man and has been good to you. Your father thinks real highly of him."

He nodded. "Yeah, I know. I'm happy they get along. I wish you and my mom would make a better effort."

"Oh now, let's not go down that route. I tried honey, I really did."

He shook his head and held up his hands. "It's okay, Sabrina, it's all good. My Mom is a force to be reckoned with."

"Now that, I agree with." She smiled, turned, and walked back out of the room. "Invite Lexi over later for dinner, if you like. I'm doing a crab boil!"

"Where the hell did you get crab from?" He called back.

"I've got friends Bobby Ray! I know people!" She laughed. He leaned against the counter and pulled out his phone. He pulled up Lexi's name and smiled at her picture before texting her.

Hey beautiful. I miss you. What are you doing later? My parents are having a crab boil and invited you over.

He pressed send and shoved it back in his pocket.

He thought about kissing her, making love to her, and just holding her in his arms again. He wanted to wake up next to her again and planned to do just that. He knew he was falling in love with her and he knew she felt the same way about him. That thought made him smile.

He finished the Dr. Pepper and ran up the stairs, two at a time, to his bedroom. He shut the door and turned on Pandora on his phone, then set it to the blue tooth and it played through the speakers in his room.

Old school country, as he called it, played through his room. *Travis Tritt's* "T-R-O-U-B-L-E" came on and he grinned. He turned up the sound and moved across the floor to the music, singing along. He grabbed boxers and socks from his dresser, a polo, and jeans from the closet. He headed toward the bathroom to shower and clean up.

Closing the bathroom door, his phone chimed when a text message from Lexi came through.

There's been a change of events and we need to talk. Everything is fine, no need to worry. I'm looking forward to kissing your sexy lips again tonight. :) Call me as soon as you can.

CHAPTER 13

*R*obert stepped out of the shower and dried his body off. He wrapped the towel around his waist and wiped his hand over the mirror. He looked at himself in the mirror then slowly ran a hand down his face. He turned his cheeks side to side, catching glimpses of the stubble growing. "I think Lexi likes it, except for the burn it gives her. Nope, not worth it. It's coming off."

He lathered up his face and turned on the water then began to shave. A few minutes later he rinsed, dried his face, and put on after shave, deodorant, and Hugo Boss cologne.

Robert walked back toward his bedroom, picking up the stereo remote from the end table. He clicked the power button and music from the preset station began to play. He dressed himself then glanced at his phone. A light flashed alerting him to a message. Seeing Lexi's name he grinned... until he saw *change of events* and *call me as soon as you can.*

He turned off Pandora and pressed dial. He heard background noises when she picked up. It sounded like she was outside, or it was windy.

"Hey there, good looking!" She giggled into the phone. "Miss me, yet?"

"Baby, I miss you the moment we're apart." And he meant it. "What's going on? What change of events?"

Lexi went into details on what Abby told her earlier. "She invited him to her party because, you know, they're best friends and shit." She sighed into the phone.

"If you don't want to go, we don't have to."

"Well, Abby made a good point. She said I can't let him dictate or rule where I go or not. Well, something like that, but her point in the matter was made. Eventually, I might be in the same room with him and I might as well get it over with while I have a hot piece of ass on my arm."

He chuckled. "Am I your hot piece of ass? Damn, I feel used."

She laughed. "You love it."

"That I do." He grinned and sat down on his bed. "Are you driving or something? There's a lot of wind or air blowing or something."

"Oh that's the air in my head trying to escape."

"What? Oh damn, woman!" Robert laughed out loud.

"Yes, I'm driving. I have clothes in my car and I'm on my way there actually."

"Really? Are you driving over naked with said clothes?" His brows rose. "I just got out of the shower, but I could be persuaded to take another one."

"Hmm... I might like that."

"Oh then, I'm definitely persuaded!" He chuckled. "How long till you're here? I'll send Dad and Sabrina out."

"About twenty minutes, I think. Give or take."

"See you soon, baby. Get here so I can see you naked that much sooner!" He heard her laugh then they said their good-byes.

He pulled on his clothes and headed downstairs. After grabbing money from his wallet and he went looking for his dad. "Go somewhere, anywhere. Just get outta here." He grinned.

"Wow, I like being paid off." He pushed the money back to his son. "No need. I'll see you in the morning."

"Thanks, Pop. I'm used to living in a dorm and not worrying about parents and shit. If you want, I can get an apartment while I'm..."

"I'll not have my son living away while he's on vacation. This house is as much yours as it is mine. Understood?"

"Yes, sir." Robert smiled. "Lexi will be here soon. I'll see y'all later."

"Treat that girl right, honey," Sabrina called as she walked into the room. "We like her."

"Yes, ma'am." He smiled then back inside with intentions to pick up his room.

Robert heard their voices fade some then the doors shut behind them. He grinned and took the stairs back up. He pulled on his pants but left his shirt hanging on its hanger. He padded back downstairs barefoot and looked out the window when he heard Lexi pull up.

When she got out of her car, he grinned. She still had on her tack store uniform and knew she'd need a shower. "Oh I can't wait for this." He rubbed his hands together with a devious grin.

He opened the door for her as she approached and noticed her eyes widen as she stared at his bare chest. Her features changed from happy to 'oh damn'. He chuckled and stood to the side.

She walked through the door and kept her eyes on his chest. "So, this is what you look like with lights on?" She ran her free hand down his chest then looked up at him with a smile. "Good god, it should be a crime to be as sexy as you are." She stood on her toes and kissed him.

Robert grabbed her hips and pulled her flush against him. His tongue wrestled with hers for dominance. She whimpered softly against his lips and he grinned. "Get your ass upstairs." He grinned and when she turned, he smacked her ass.

"Damn, baby!" She laughed and ran up the stairs. Robert

locked the front door then followed up behind her. He went to his bedroom first and found her unpacking an overnight back. "You planned this out or what?" He chuckled and came up behind her. He wrapped his arms around her body and pulled her against him. His hands moved over her breasts and he squeezed them.

She leaned into his chest and let her head rest on his shoulder. She laid her hands over his as he kneaded against her flesh. "I missed you."

He kissed on her neck and he spoke just under her ear. "I missed you." He turned her around and claimed her lips. His hands grabbed her shirt and he untucked it then pulled it over her head. He looked down to her black, sheer bra with an appreciative smile. "Damn baby, hot bra. Do the panties match?"

She grinned and unbuttoned her pants. She kicked off her boots and pushed her pants down. After stepping out of them, she stood straight and smiled. "Sure do. You like?" She turned around and looked over her shoulder.

Robert bit his knuckles and shook his head. "Dammit, you're hot." He closed the distance to her and kissed her shoulder. Leaning around her, his left hand took her chin and brought her head back as he kissed her neck. His other hand wrapped around her body and massaged one of her breasts.

She breathed heavily against him as he took possession of her body. "Robert, please..." is all she could get out. Her panties were wet and she needed to get them off.

"Yes?" He asked in her softly in her ear. "Tell me what you want to do."

"Oh god," she breathed. She closed her eyes as his hand moved over her stomach, landing over her panties. He gently grabbed her between the legs and listened to her gasp. He then pushed her panties to the side and slid a finger between her folds. He teased her and nibbled on her ear as she gasped again. "Oh my god, this, lots of this. Shit Robert, don't stop."

"Mmm," he groaned against her neck and his hand clinched

her head against his shoulder. "I want to fuck you in the shower. Right now." She quivered in his arms. He continued to move his fingers between her folds then tilted her head over just enough to kiss her.

She wrapped one of her arms around his neck and tried to hold onto him, until her legs almost gave out underneath her. He removed his hand from between her legs then turned her back around to face him. He kissed her hard and she grabbed at his pants, unbuttoning them as quickly as she could. She grabbed at the waistline and pushed them down his body until he was able to kick them off.

Robert moved his hands down the back of her thighs then lifted her up. She wrapped her legs around his waist and he carried her toward the bathroom.

~

*B*laine pulled off the main interstate and headed toward Abby's place. The sun was already beginning to set and he knew he'd see Lexi tonight. He wanted to surprise her and take her off guard. He wanted to kiss her and feel her lips around his dick again. He wanted to fuck her once more before he got back out on the road.

But if she'd hooked up with another guy, it was going to be harder for him to get her back. He hadn't had to fight for a good piece of ass in a long, long time. Hell, getting it thrown at you... what's to fight for? He'd enjoyed the chase, enjoyed the hunt. She was the fox and he was the hunter. He planned on catching her and taking her down.

Before going to the party, he needed something extra, something to help take the edge off. He pulled off the main strip and headed toward the hood... or at least that's what he remembered this area being. The middle income looking houses began shifting into what people would stereotype as the projects. He reached over and double-checked the locks on his doors. "Well, I can see shit hasn't changed."

The old dilapidated buildings looked like they were standing on their last legs. Paint was chipped on the outer walls and a few windows were boarded up with cardboard and duct tape. A bad storm or strong wind would be all it took to knock down the fixed income homes and apartments.

He slowed down and looked for a dealer. Pulling up to a light he looked around, then jumped when someone knocked on his window. He pressed the window button and cracked it slightly.

"You buying?" The Hispanic male asked him. He smelled as if he hadn't brushed his teeth or showered in a month. He had on a black t-shirt that had holes in it and dirty jeans.

Blaine waved the air in front of him and made a disgusting face. "Yeah man, you got any X or coke?"

"What the fuck you think this is, homie? You in da hood. Don't act like your white boy ass is better than me!" He stood back up and thrashed his arms in a way to show offense. "Driving a car like dat here will get you 'jacked, man."

"Look man, meant no disrespect. I'm buying. You selling or not?" He didn't want to bullshit around. Blaine wanted out of there as fast as possible. He wasn't stupid, although driving a Caddie in this part of town wasn't the brightest of ideas, either. This fucker could pull a gun out and shoot him. Then where would that leave him? No band and no piece of ass from Lexi.

"Yeah. You 5-0?"

"Fuck no. Here's the cash. Now hand it over! Ain't got all night." Blaine held it to the window, just out of reach. The dealer pulled out two baggies; one with a few pills the other with a vial of soft white powder. He presented them to the window as Blaine pushed his cash through. "See ya. Take a fucking shower." He rolled up his window and pressed the gas pedal.

The man yelled back, "Fuck you, man!" He pushed the cash in his pocket and walked back to the sidewalk.

Blaine's heartbeat sped up in his chest and he inhaled deeply, trying to slow it down. "Fuck me!" He laughed and shook it off. He pulled out onto the main strip and headed toward Abby's farmhouse for the party that would welcome him back to town. This would be a party he and Lexi wouldn't soon forget.

He pulled up to a stoplight and looked over at the two small baggies next to him on the passenger seat. There was barely an ounce of the powder and Blaine snarled. "Fucked up piece of shit shorted me!"

The light changed green and Blaine gunned it. His tires squealed on the asphalt and he had it in his head to hunt down that dealer. Maybe if he shouted, threw a few punches, he'd get his fair share. Then he shook his head and continued driving. A memory of Lexi returned to him.

"Why must you drive so fast?" She'd ask.

He'd smirked at her. "Why, does it scare you?"

"Fucking bitch will be scared tonight if I have anything to do with it. She'll never leave me again."

Abby's drive came into view and he turned down the dirt road. He could see the bonfire had already started and music was blaring. He smirked hearing his own tune, *The One That Got Away*. He parked and turned off the headlights, then reached for the vial of powder. He pulled out his small coke spoon and scooped some out, then snorted it. He wiped his nose and sniffed a few more times. He grabbed the X and stuffed it into his pocket.

Blaine left his car and began feeling the high from the coke. He smiled and walked into the crowd to a few claps on the back, a few hugs, and people asking how life was on the road. He answered questions and signed a few autographs. He continued telling his former classmates, "Hey man, it's still me. I haven't changed that much."

It was about that time he looked across the bonfire and saw Abby. She was hard to miss. She'd happened to find the shortest skirt imaginable and yet, still cover her ass. He smirked and rubbed his crotch. The short black skirt... if you would even call it that, was paired with a red top fitted to her body. Her toned arms were exposed. He appreciated a fit girl. His eyes scanned down her bare legs to her platform sandals. This woman had legs up to her neck. He walked around the bonfire, not wanting to be seen.

He stepped up behind Abby and whispered next to her ear, "You got a hug for your old friend?"

She smiled then turned around. Her long blond hair flowed down her back and her dark brown eyes took in the sight of him. "Well, if it isn't mister rock star himself," Abby smirked at him. She wanted to look perfect for tonight and the fact that he was checking out her legs didn't go unnoticed. It also told her: mission accomplished. She looked him over and admired his black fitted t-shirt, how it clung to his strong, tattooed arms. Then to the waist that she wanted to desperately run her tongue over. His jeans were nicely snug in all the right places. She never understood why guys would ever wear skinny jeans.

Her eyes trailed back up and she shifted in her step. She was ready for Blaine right now. She'd waited long enough and continued to play his game. She stepped closer and ran her mani-cured fingers up his chest, feeling his muscles flex. "It's about time you got here," she whispered. She leaned in and wrapped her arms around his neck, hugging him to her. She pressed her body firmly against his and could feel his erection pressing right at the bottom of her skirt.

Blaine cleared his throat then grabbed Abby's arms, pulling her off him. "Not here," he whispered. "Don't act like we're together!" When she frowned, he touched her chin and lifted her face up. "Give me time to make rounds and wait for Lexi and her fuck of the moment to show up; then I'll take you upstairs and fuck your brains out." He watched her body shiver in excitement. "That's what I thought." He leaned in and kissed her cheek. When he pulled away, he raised his voice, "Abby, always great to see you kid! Where's Lexi? She coming?"

She had to play her part. She nodded with a smile, while deep inside she hated knowing he was still pining for her. *What the fuck does she have that I don't? He would probably tell me his heart. Whatever. Fuck that. He's mine.* She smiled again, "She should be here soon enough. I'm positive she'll be very excited to see you."

Blaine raised a brow then turned away from her and grabbed a beer from a nearby cooler.

~

*R*obert pulled the car to a stop in the middle of town and looked over to Lexi once more. "You're positive about this? You really want to go?"

She nodded. "Yes, Abby is right. How can I ever move forward if I can't even be in the same vicinity as he is? I'm over him and his shit." She smiled and slipped her hand into his. She lifted it to her lips and kissed it. "Besides, I have you now. You're my man. He was just a boy."

Robert nodded. "You might have an opportunity to tell him that then if you like." He ran his thumb lightly over her hand. "The moment you're ready to go, give me the word and we're out of there. Okay?"

Lexi smiled and leaned over to steal a kiss. "You're so good to me. Thank you."

The light turned green and he squeezed her hand then took off under the light. His hands were squeezing the steering wheel a little too tightly, not liking the idea of being at this party with Blaine making an appearance. He had no idea what Blaine could be capable of or what lies he might try to tell Lexi. He glanced over at her once more with a soft smile. "You trust me, don't you?"

"What?" She smiled. "Of course I do. Why do you ask?"

"I just want to make sure that no matter what happens tonight, you know I have your back… and your front." He winked.

She giggled. "Bobby Ray, we'll be fine. I'll be fine. Makayla and Abby will both be there. They won't let anything happen to me."

"You're sure about that?" He knew Makayla would watch out for her... as long as Conner didn't have her in a lip lock. As for Abby, he didn't trust her. There was something about her he didn't like, but he couldn't quite figure it out. It could have been all his years around politics, and having the ability to sniff out the wrong guy to associate himself around; there was no telling.

"I'm positive." She smiled and squeezed his hand as the blaze of the bonfire glowed over the horizon.

~

*A*bby walked into her house and refilled the cooler with ice. She bent over to pick up a few cubes that had fallen onto the floor when she felt wind blow against her body. She turned and looked over her shoulder to find Blaine watching her... well, watching her ass. "You like what you see, honey?"

"Damn woman, are you wearing panties?" He stepped in closer, moved his hand over her back, and pulled her skirt up. He grinned and allowed her to stand. She adjusted her skirt back down with a grin. "Nice, commando. Hot as fuck!"

"Let me take this back outside and..."

He cut her off. "No. Bathroom, now. I'm fucking that beautiful mouth of yours then sinking deep inside you."

She watched his eyes light up and she bit her lip. "Wow, you know how to talk to a girl, don't you?" Abby took his hand and led him through the den, toward the guest bathroom. She knocked on the door and felt Blaine's lips on her neck. She gasped and pressed her fingers against the door. "Blaine, baby, hang on." She checked the handle then pushed the door open.

They walked in and Blaine quickly shut the door behind them. He pulled Abby roughly toward him and kissed her hard. His tongue ring rubbed roughly against her soft pallet and occasionally, it clinked against her teeth.

He pushed her up against the wall, moved his hands down to her breasts, and squeezed them hard. "I want you to suck my dick. Now." He moved his hands to his pants and suddenly, Abby grabbed him.

"No, allow me." She in turn pushed him against the counter and roughly unbuckled his belt then unbuttoned his jeans, pushing them down his legs. She grabbed his boxers, yanked them down, and her nails scratched him in the process.

"Fuck woman! That fucking hurt! No marks!"

"Oh hush, you might like being hurt." She grabbed his length and licked the tip.

He growled then took hold of her blond hair in a tight fist. He watched her lips part and he grabbed his dick and pressed it to her lips. He smirked as he watched her take it completely. "Fuck woman," he growled.

CHAPTER 14

"*L*exi!" Makayla called across the yard and jogged up to her friend, then wrapped her in a big hug. "I've missed you." She glared at Robert. "Someone's been keeping you busy."

"Oh hun, don't blame him. It's my fault, too," she told her friend. "Trust me when I say it's been well worth it." She smiled.

Makayla noticed how it touched her eyes then she looked at Robert again with a smirk. "I see you've been busy getting acquainted."

He chuckled. "Yeah, something like that." He wrapped an arm around Lexi's shoulders and pulled her close. She, in turn, wrapped an arm around his waist.

Makayla looked between the two of them with raised brows. "So, are you two an item now?"

They looked to each other with a smile then he shrugged. She turned and nodded to Makayla.

"OhMyGod! This is great!" She squealed and Conner came up behind her.

"Hey, Bobby Ray. Good to see ya again." He shook his hand with a smile. "Do I need to pull her in?" He chuckled.

"Whatever!" Makayla slapped his arm playfully. "I'm just happy for my best friend and my favorite cousin! Let me have this moment."

"Women," Conner chuckled.

Robert shook his head. "Baby, you want a drink?"

She nodded. "Yeah, get me a beer, or whatever Abby has here."

"Cool. Makayla?"

She looked at her boyfriend with a raised brow. "Why can't you do that for me?"

"Because I already have you; I'm no longer trying to impress your sexy ass." He smacked said ass and when she squealed, he jumped back to avoid getting slapped.

"You should never stop!" She exclaimed.

Lexi reached for her. "C'mon, let's go walk around. I want to see who's here."

Makayla knew that meant code for 'let's see if Blaine has already graced everyone with his presence'. "I think he's here, honey. I heard people talking about him, but I haven't seen him yet."

"Oh, perfect," she sighed. "Abby did make a good point to me, though."

The two walked away from Robert and Conner. "When did you see Abby," she asked.

"Oh she came by the tack store the other day to warn me Blaine would be here. She said she invited him because," she air quoted, *"he's my friend and I want to welcome him home."*

"Oh god, are you serious?" Makayla made a disgusting face.

Lexi grinned. "I'm glad you see it my way."

"Okay, but what did she say that you agreed with? It couldn't have been him coming here."

"No, definitely not that. She told me in order to get past what we had, it would be best just to face him… like get it over with. It was something like that, but honestly, she had a point."

Makayla looked the other way and watched a few of the party-goers take shots. One girl looked a bit woozy and she stumbled slightly. She continued looking around the party then asked, "Speaking of Abby, have you seen her?"

"Nope, just got here." Lexi looked back across the lawn and found Robert talking with a few guys they knew from high school. Funny how time changes people. In their mid-twenties, these guys looked like they had gained fifty pounds and gone bald overnight. She couldn't help but grin when Robert turned to catch her gaze. He winked at her and she blew him a kiss.

"Eww, god Lexi, don't do that."

"Oh like it's any different with Conner?"

"Actually, yeah it is. Bobby Ray is my cousin." She shuddered, giving it effect. Lexi laughed. "Well, let me go see if I can hunt queen bee down. You'll be okay out here?"

"You bet." She smiled. I need to play catch up with a few girls from high school and talk to them about College Station.

"Oh, are you going back?" Makayla asked.

"I'm not sure yet. Mama's been acting kinda funny lately about things. I don't know what it is, but I'll figure it out." She smiled. "Don't worry about it."

"I always do. It's just the two of you."

"No, I have you, and now, it looks like I have Bobby Ray. You know, he's talking of transferring here to finish school."

Makayla smiled. "So he told me."

"What? When did he tell you that?" Lexi grinned and crossed her arms over her body.

"Oh... maybe the day after your big date?"

"But that was like weeks ago!" She exclaimed.

Makayla nodded. "I know," she winked. "Okay, I'm off to find Abby. Keep your phone handy in case I get lost in her house. It's huge!"

Lexi wondered how often Abby ever had to do without what she wanted, when she wanted it. Growing up in a home where her father was wealthy put Abby in a class above everyone else... at least that is what Abby used to tell them as children.

A grin formed on Lexi's lips. "My phone will be right here." She patted her shorts pocket.

"Alright, I'm going in!" Makayla shook her head and turned toward the house.

∾

"*O*h god, Blaine!" Abby grabbed onto his arms while he held her slender legs against his chest. "Harder!"

"Fuck woman!" He pumped faster inside her and Abby screamed his name again.

"Abby?" A voice sounded on the other side of the door then the handle jiggled.

"Shit! Didn't you lock the door?" She asked him then moaned again. He continued to thrust against her and her head hung back. "Fuck, you feel good!"

"I don't know if I fucking locked it! If she hears you moan and comes in anyway, we'll have a fucking three-some." He thrust harder against her.

"Blaine!" She yelled out his name.

"Fuck yeah, say my name bitch!"

"Blaine! Fuck me!" Abby's voice screamed throughout the bathroom.

"What the hell?" Makayla opened the door with a horror struck face. "Abby! How could you?!" She then looked at Blaine and shook her head. "You are a piece of fucking shit! You don't surprise me by anything you do, but this? Fucking one of Lexi's best friends?" She turned to Abby and snarled. "I can't BELIEVE you!" She shook her head again. "You fucking deserve each other!" She slammed the door shut then turned the other way.

"Shit!" Abby yelled. "She'll go down and tell Lexi!"

"Fuck," Blaine pulled out of her and removed the condom. "Go fucking find her man and tell him I was in here with her, fucking her."

She stared at him for a moment in disbelief. "What?" Abby's voice came out in a whisper.

"GO!"

Abby flinched then she grabbed her clothes and pulled them back on. She stood there for a moment then felt herself fighting back tears. "I thought you wanted to be with me."

"Woman, I can't be with someone like you. You expect shit from me and I can't give that. I'm on the road. I play music. Fucking women is what I do. Now go tell him I was in here with her!"

The venom in his voice was perfectly clear. He may as well have slapped her in the face. Abby opened the bathroom door and walked out, feeling like she was doing the walk of shame.

Blaine came out of the bathroom next and quickly swallowed the X from his pocket, then snorted more coke. He wiped his nose and found Lexi inside the house pouring a beer. He walked up behind her and hoped he didn't smell like sex... like he knew Abby would. "Hey, beautiful. Came all this way to see me?"

~

"*B*obby Ray, there you are!" Abby walked up to him, tugging at the bottom of her skirt.

He turned and looked her over and his lips turned in a frown. "Where's the bottom half of your outfit?"

"This IS my outfit." She grinned. "Don't you like it?" She put her hands to her hips and leaned to the right, popping her hip out.

"Honestly? No." She blanched. "I like my women a little more conservative. Not looking like she's half dressed. But hey, if this works for you, you don't need my approval."

"I'm not sure whether I should be offended by that, or flattered for your concern."

"Oh, I'm not concerned about what you wear." He knew now

135

what he didn't like about her. She came across conceited and shallow; two traits that definitely turned him off.

He started to walk past her but not before Abby reached out for his arm. "Bobby Ray, wait!" She turned him back around. "I came to find you for a reason. It's Lexi."

He glared at the woman and raised a brow. *Oh this outta be good,* he thought to himself. "What about her?"

"You know about the history between her and Blaine, right?" Robert nodded and crossed his arms, waiting for her to continue. "Well, they are getting re-acquainted right now."

"We knew he'd be here, you told her yourself. So, I'm sure she's capable of having an adult conversation with her *ex*," putting emphasis on the word.

"Umm," Abby twisted her fingers in a nervous gesture. "That's just it, Bobby Ray. I found them in the bathroom. I went to go use the bathroom and well? I heard noises on the other side. I smiled at first because someone was getting lucky. I was curious so I checked the handle and it was unlocked. I looked inside and he had her on the counter, naked... fucking her."

Robert's face turned red and he grit his teeth. "What?" He growled.

"I'm so sorry to be the one to tell you this. She's back with Blaine, honey. He came back for her and he got what he wanted." She stepped closer to him and rested her hand on his forearm. "I'm here for you honey, I can take you home, if you like." She gave him doe eyes and stepped closer.

Robert wasn't looking at Abby; he wasn't looking at anything. When her words finally sunk in, he looked around for Lexi, for Makayla, for anyone. No one was around. When he felt Abby brush against him, he looked down. "What the fuck do you think you're doing?"

"Excuse me?" She exclaimed. "I'm trying to be here for you."

"By doing what? Feel me up when my girl is fucking her ex?

Real nice, Abby." He removed her hands from him, turned, and walked away.

Conner walked out of the house and yelled over at Robert to slow down. He jogged to catch him then pulled him off to the side. "Hey man, you seen Lexi or Makayla? I can't find either of them around."

"Where the fuck is Blaine?" Robert asked him. He looked at the young man and everything kind was gone from his eyes.

"Dude, what the fuck?" Conner glared at Robert. "What the fuck happened?"

"I just heard that Blaine had Lexi in the bathroom."

Conner's eyes widened. "What the fuck? Who told you that?"

"Abby," Robert lowered his gaze to the ground. "I don't want to believe it. I really don't." He looked back at Conner again. "They have history..."

Conner held up his hands and shook his head. "Let's go inside and see if we can find her. Don't believe anything that slut has to say."

Robert raised a brow. "So you're not a fan of Abby's?"

"Fuck, no." Conner walked toward the back door entrance and turned back to him. "Not after she tried to fuck me."

Robert nodded, "Explains a lot." He followed his friend inside and they looked around. People were talking, the music was loud, and someone was doing a keg stand. "Do you see her?" Robert raised his voice to be heard over the music.

Conner shook his head then did a double take, "There she is!" He pointed across the room to the other door that lead to the front area of the house. Behind her was Blaine.

Robert's lip curled and heat fired inside of him. "I'm leaving. You can take Lexi home?"

Conner looked him over and finally nodded. "Sure. You don't think she actually did it, do you?"

Blaine slipped an arm around Lexi's shoulder and pulled her

close. "Ask her when you see her." Robert turned, pulled his keys from his pocket, and headed toward his truck.

Abby stood on the porch of her house, watching him leave.

Conner followed him then stood next to her. "Have you seen Makayla?"

"No," Abby looked at him and wiped a tear from her eye.

"Are you crying? You alright?"

Abby smiled and nodded. "Yeah, I'll be fine. Thank you for asking." She turned to walk back inside the house while mumbling, "Fuck! I'm an awful person and am going straight to hell."

She walked into her house and went to her bedroom, shutting the door. She made her way to her bathroom and looked at herself in the mirror. "When did I become... this?" She gripped the counter and began to sob. She suddenly ran to the toilet and vomited.

∾

*L*exi froze in her step. Her eyes moved first then she set down the keg tube. She took a deep breath and found Blaine standing right behind her. Damn, did he look like sex on a fucking stick.

He smiled at her and looked her body over with a tilt of his head. "Damn baby, you look good." He stepped in closer and reached for her.

"What do you think you're doing?" She asked and stepped away. "I'm not your baby, either."

"Since when?" He grinned and stepped closer to her. He noticed a wall coming up close behind her and he'd have her trapped. "I love you, baby. You know that."

"You have a fucked up way to showing it. Oh, let me guess, you slept with all those women to help you sleep at night because you were so hung up on me. Is that it?"

He furrowed his brows. "Not far from the truth, but no. To be perfectly honest, do you know how hard it is, day after fucking day, to have pussy thrown in your face? Every single fucking day, Lexi! It's only a matter of time before you break down and either taste it or fuck it." He shrugged. "I did a little of both. Trust me when I tell you, I always thought of you."

Lexi thought she might retch on his words as her back hit the wall behind her. She shook her head. "Do you actually believe what's coming out of your mouth? I mean, seriously Blaine! Leave me alone!" She side stepped him and started to walk outside to find Robert.

Blaine followed her out and quickly slipped an arm around her shoulder and pulled her close to him. "Don't deny me, Lexi. I want you. You'll give yourself to me willingly or I'll just take you."

"What, you'll rape me? Real nice, Blaine. That's a whole new low, even for you." She shook herself from his arm and made it as far as the door.

He suddenly grabbed her and forced her against the wall. He leaned in and grabbed her throat, but didn't choke her. He watched her eyes widen and enjoyed the control he had over her. He smirked then quickly leaned in and kissed her.

Next thing Blaine knew he was on the ground, groaning. Lexi stepped over his body and yelled at him, "FUCK YOU, BLAINE!" She kicked him in his ass then stormed out of the den.

"I'll take your fucking farm, you whore!" He yelled back. The crowd in the house became quiet.

Lexi stopped and turned back to him as he was getting to his feet. She walked back up to him and slapped him hard across the face. "Fuck you."

"Yeah, fuck me. You want to keep your farm? You're mine and no one else's. You got that?" He smirked and rubbed his sore groin. Blue balls from not cumming with Abby then being kneed by his ex… not exactly how he saw this going down.

"What the HELL do you know about my farm?"

"Enough to know your mother is going into foreclosure unless she comes up with twenty grand to pay her debt." He gave her a sadistic grin. "I happen to have more than enough to share with your mother, and I can help her. If not, I'll take the deed, and your land. Then you," he touched her face, "belong to me."

"I'm not fucking property you can buy or auction, you asshole!" She slapped his hand away.

"Fine. Have you it your way. One call to my lawyer and the paperwork starts."

"You wouldn't dare!" She yelled.

Right about that time, Makayla came up behind her and took her arms. "Lexi, let's go. He's not worth it."

"Oh, she's not done here," he told Makayla. "She's done when I say she's done."

"You don't fucking own her, you piece of shit and you definitely cannot tell me what to do. So go shove your dick in your ass and fuck yourself." She wrapped her arm around Lexi and escorted her toward the door.

"Last chance, sweetheart. Me or lose your farm."

"My mother wouldn't have to think twice if it came to this. You can fucking have it."

Lexi and Makayla walked out of the room to whispers and accusations. Others turned toward Blaine with a newfound hatred. A tall, buff man walked up to Blaine and poked him in the chest. "Takes a real man to fuck with a woman like that. Time for you to fucking leave, rock star."

Others cheered on the tall man and Blaine growled. "I'm not scared of you or anyone else here! Who the fuck are you anyway? Football quarterback jock? Yeah go back to high school!" He turned away from the guy and talked to the crowd. "I'll take any one of you on!" As soon as he turned back to the tall, buff man, a fist made its way into his jaw, with a resounding crack.

Blaine was thrown to the floor and he groaned, grabbing his face. "Fuck, man!"

"Time for you to fucking leave, rock star. Don't make me say it again." The man reached down, grabbed Blaine by his shirt, and pulled him to his feet as if he were a nothing but a rag doll. "Now, go." He threw him toward the door and Blaine landed against the wall with a loud smack.

People around them laughed and he sneered. "Fuck all y'all! I'm rich and in a rock band! What are you? You're here in fucking TexASS trying to make a living. You remember that when you see my album hit number one!" He turned and walked out of the house, but not before Abby tripped him.

Blaine fell face first onto the front porch with a thud and a grunt. "What in the FUCK, woman?" He turned over and found himself staring up at a double barrel shot gun. His eyes widened and he looked from the barrels up to a very pissed off Abby.

She proceeded to stand over him, straddling his body with her now clothed legs. She cocked her rifle with a single pump. "I'm telling her exactly what you did and had me do, ass clown. Now get off my property before I shoot your ass."

He looked from Abby to the gun, then back to her again. He looked to the people staring at him in bewilderment. Rage began to consume him and he slid on his back away from the gun barrel. "You shoot me, you'll go to prison, you whore." Blaine's words were pure hatred.

Abby gritted her teeth and began to take a step forward when the tall, buff man from earlier reappeared at her back. He glared down at Blaine then rested his hands on her shoulders. "I suggest you apologize to the lady then be on your way." Abby smiled at his words, hoping they sunk into Blaine's small mind.

"Lady? Apologize? She was just in there sucking my dick, then went and told my girl's fuck buddy I was screwing *her*! You call that a fucking lady?"

"Oh, that's it!" Abby yelled. "Get off my property! You won't get another warning, Blaine!"

He scooted back a little farther then quickly got to his feet.

"I don't give a fuck what she did or didn't do to you. The lady said to leave; now get the fuck out of here before I personally remove you. Trust me," he folded his arms over his chest. "It WILL be in a box."

Blaine's eyes widened and looked around in hopes of someone, anyone, having his back. He'd left Texas so quickly and hadn't bothered looking back. Maybe he should have. He'd left Lexi high and dry with a broken heart. Maybe he should have accepted the inevitable and just broken it off.

He now stared at Abby. Seeing the friendship... or whatever this between them had been, was now gone. He finally nodded and shoved his hands in his pockets and his fingers felt the plastic baggies holding his drugs. He lowered his gaze and stepped off the porch. "Alright, I'm leaving. You made your fucking point." Blaine turned and walked toward his car, the crowd watching still silent.

As he slid into his front seat and started up his car, he looked up one last time and saw Abby crying. The tall buff guy was holding her close. Did they know each other? Was she fucking him, too? "Aww hell." He shook his head then watched her pull away. She took out her phone and most likely, following through with what she promised: to confess everything to Lexi.

CHAPTER 15

*P*ulling out of Abby's driveway, Blaine headed back into town. The plastic bags that had been in his pocket were now sitting on the passenger seat next to him. He ran his hand through his hair and cursed at himself for making this night much worse than he'd actually intended.

"I wanted to fuck Lexi one last time. I wanted her to be mine, hell she IS mine! Then that mother fucker, Bobby Ray, had to come in to her life and taken her from me. Nah, fuck this shit." He snatched one of the baggies and felt the ecstasy inside it. He opened the bag and popped them all into his mouth. He wasn't sure how many there were, maybe five, maybe seven. He grabbed his beer and swallowed them down.

He pulled the car over to the side of the road. He might be high, he might be stoned off his ass, but he was smart enough to get off the damn road. He looked down at the coke next to him and licked his bottom lip. He pulled out his coke spoon and opened the bag of coke. He gently laid it out on the center console.

He stared down at the white substance, then without thinking of his actions or consequences, he began snorting a spoonful of the coke at a time. He snorted it all as fast as he could until only residue was left. He was pissed at the world and didn't want to remember anything. *Fuck them, fuck Lexi, and fuck that mother fucker who fucked her. Fuck the band and fuck my fucking life.*

Blaine stepped out of his car and stared up at the night sky. The high was more than he had ever experienced. He stumbled and continued to stare at the stars until they began to blink at him. He laughed and began to twirl in a circle.

A loud horn sounded as a car went by him. He didn't care. He walked down the road when the coke began to take effect... that and the X.

Blaine held his head and screamed from the pain, from the high, from feeling like he was losing himself. In that moment, everything went black and he fell to the asphalt of the road, face first, and passed out.

❦

"Mother fucker!" Robert hit his steering wheel a few times on his drive back home. He rolled the windows down and welcomed the chill in the air. He yelled a few times as the anger and rage overwhelmed him.

"Let's go to the party, she said. I need to face him sometime, she said. Well facing him and fucking him are two VERY different things, Lexi Griffin!" He turned on the radio and turned the volume up as loud as it would go. He wanted the music to drown out what he was feeling. Unfortunately, hearing *George Strait* sing about *The Chair* wasn't doing it for him.

He turned the station to rock and Metallica played through the speakers. Old school rock, *Master of Puppets* to be exact, is what he needed. His phone, next to him, lit up with Makayla's number, but he ignored it.

As he made it home and turned into the driveway, he turned down the music and parked the car. He hit the steering wheel a few more times and yelled out once. He rested his head on his hands and sobbed for a moment. The last time he gave his heart, she cheated on him. Here it was happening again exactly the same way.

Robert and his then girlfriend were in the same place at the same time. He walked in on her getting it on with her ex. He never would have though Lexi would have done the same.

"Bobby Ray?" Sabrina's voice sounded next to him.

He sat up and wiped his face on his arms. "Yeah, I'm cool." He opened the door and slid out.

"You had me in a fright, son! I heard you yell and came running out."

"Shit, I'm so sorry. I didn't mean to." He let his head drop between his shoulders and sighed.

"Come here," she pulled him close to her. Robert leaned into her and felt himself letting go. He pulled his stepmother closer and cried into her shoulder. "Oh honey, come on, tell me what happened. Let me help."

"Lexi… She, she was caught having sex with her ex at the party." He pulled back and wiped his face again.

"Oh no… Robert, I'm so sorry." She reached up and wiped his tears, then touched his face. "Did you catch her?"

He shook his head. "No, it was her friend, Abby. I didn't believe it at first; then I saw her and Blaine together." He shook his head. "I couldn't stay there and watch that unfold."

"I see. Well, come inside. I'll make us some coffee." She took his arm and they began walking toward the house. "And you're positive that is what happened? Did you talk to her?"

"I didn't need to. I saw him with her. I saw him put his arms around her." He sniffed and sighed. "If it's all the same to you, I'd rather just go to bed. I'll find the first flight out in the morning. Thank you for having me, and thank you for being an amazing woman for my dad. Hell, and for me too… Mom."

She smiled. "Mom? Well, thank you, honey. Okay, then you get on up to bed. I'll have that coffee ready in the morning; we'll figure this mess out." She touched his face once more. "Love you, kiddo. Try to sleep."

He nodded and tried to smile, but it came across as more of a grimace. He took the stairs two at a time and went into his room. His phone lit up again with Makayla's number. He sent it to voicemail then turned it off. He tossed it on the dresser, removed his boots, and climbed into bed.

He stared at the ceiling, trying to understand what had happened, what had gone wrong. "I thought she was falling for me. How could she throw that away? Fuck this shit." He turned on his side and stared at the wall for a bit. Images of Lexi moved through his head: her lips, her body, the way she kissed him, the way they made love... all of it. He forced his eyes closed and made himself think about school and what he has coming up next semester. He knew he'd be helping his stepfather, gaining the political experience for school. He also knew he would be on the campaign trail soon. He planned to start running for offices in college and having a broken heart wasn't a way to begin his career. He sighed and allowed sleep to begin taking him under.

~

*T*he next morning, Robert came awake with thoughts of Lexi. He wanted to see her again, feel her lips on his, his arms around her body. As his body began waking up, so did his mind. The events of last night came rushing back and he felt his heart break inside his chest.

His hands covered his face and he groaned. "Fuck..." Robert sat up and looked across the room to his dresser. A few pictures of him and Lexi were on his mirror. They were smiling and happy. He stood up and walked over to them. He pulled them each off his mirror and tossed them into the nearby trashcan.

He grabbed his phone and turned it on. After it booted up, a green light flashed that caught his attention. He swiped his finger across it. Eighteen new voicemails, half of them from Lexi. He sighed, dropped it back onto the dresser, and headed toward the bathroom to piss and take a shower.

Robert turned on the water and stood there staring at the stream. He felt empty. He shook his head and quickly brushed his teeth. Once the steam began filling the bathroom, he stepped inside the shower, and pulled the curtain closed around him.

"What the fuck happened to us?" *Maybe you should call her and find out. No, don't call. She'll just tell you she found love with her ex again... that or she'll lie about it.* Visions of his ex haunted his mind and the excuses she would use on him for why she cheated. He sighed and began washing his hair and body. Once he finished, he stepped out to dry off.

"Bobby Ray?" Sabrina called for him from downstairs. "Breakfast is ready."

"Thanks," he called back. "Give me a minute, I'll be down." He got himself dressed in khaki shorts and a white t-shirt with the words, *University of Georgia* across the front.

"Those are fighting words, you know." The teasing from Lexi came to mind and he considered ripping the shirt from his body.

Descending the stairs, he found his dad and stepmom at the dining room table eating breakfast, sipping coffee, and reading the morning news. He plated himself some eggs, bacon, and toast then took a seat.

"Son, you alright?" His father asked as he sat his paper down.

"Yeah, Pop, I will be." Robert chewed on some bacon then sipped his coffee.

"If you're serious about leaving, I took the liberty of finding a few flights back to Georgia, although I hope you'll reconsider. I've enjoyed having you here." His father reached over and squeezed his shoulder.

Robert nodded. "Thanks Pop. I've enjoyed my time here, too. But I need to go back to finish my classes."

His father started, "It's nothing you can't finish…"

"Pop, I need to go. As much as I'd love to stay here for you and Sabrina, I can't. At least not right now."

"It's okay, son, I understand."

"Bobby Ray, she called a few times this morning," Sabrina announced. She looked up to her stepson and saw the concern on his face. "Don't worry, I only told her you made it home safely, nothing more. She doesn't know if you're headed back or not. We're leaving that up to you to tell her."

"I don't owe her shit. I have nothing to say." He lowered his gaze, his voice lit with hatred. He shoveled in a huge bite of eggs.

"Honey," she started, "it's bad to fight then just leave. Call her and see if she can…"

"No. I heard and saw enough last night. I'm good." He stood and put his plate and coffee mug in the sink. "Excuse me while I go pack. Thanks Pop, for checking flights for me." He walked out of the room and sighed out loud.

"Well, that went well," Sabrina announced.

"Hush woman. He's hurting."

"Rightfully, so. According to him, last night she got back with her ex at whatever party they went to."

Jim shook his head. "Kids, I swear. They'll grow up one day and realize this bullshit of playing games is overrated." He brought his wife's hand to his lips and kissed it. "I don't know what I would have done without you when Allison left me the way she did."

Sabrina smiled. "I knew you a long while before all that happened. We both knew she wasn't happy here. She wanted much more than being a farmer's wife could provide her."

He looked into her eyes and gave her a smile. "I love you, woman."

"I love you, too. Now, let's go get your son ready."

~

*R*obert sat on the edge of his bed and stared at his hands. He fisted them then released a few times. He felt a tear race down his cheek and he quickly swiped it away.

"Son?"

Robert looked up to his father, standing in the door frame. "Hey, Pop." He looked back down again, stood up, and walked to his closet to get his clothes.

"Son," Jim walked into the bedroom and leaned against the door to the closet. "Want to talk about it?"

"Which part? How I took her to a party where her ex would be? Knowing he was her first love? Knowing he'd try to get her back? I'm such a damn idiot!" Robert raised his voice and he felt his face turning red from the pain.

"Alright son, step out here before you hurt yourself." Jim moved back and made room for his son. "Why don't you start with telling me what happened. How did you find out what she did or didn't do?"

Robert took a deep breath then went into the details that Abby had filled him in on. How she had walked in on them in the bathroom having sex on the counter and him seeing Blaine wrap an arm around her and pull her close.

"Well, I see." Jim crossed his arms over his chest and stared at his son. "So, what are you gonna do about it?"

"What can I do? She made her choice and it wasn't me." Robert began throwing his clothes into his suitcase. "It was so stupid us getting together in the first place!"

"Do you really think she did what this girl said she did?" Jim crossed the room and touched his son's shoulder. "Stop a minute, look at me. I'm serious son. Do you really think she did this?"

"Hell, Pop I don't know. I want to say no, but I also don't understand why Abby would lie about it. I knew the history Lexi had with this Blaine asshole. Abby also attempted to make a play for me."

"This girl, Abby, was trying to make a move on you right after that happened? Don't you find that the least bit... oh, I don't know, odd?"

"Honestly? Not really. I've heard she gets around. I've also found her giving me the once over before."

Jim shook his head. "Did you at least call Lexi to hear what she had to say for herself?"

"Nope. I don't care to hear it."

"You won't give her a chance to explain or defend herself?"

"How can I? I went through this once before. I can't do it again." Robert's voice rose again.

Jim sighed, then lowered his gaze and covered his jaw with his hand. "You do what you think is best, then. Let me know when you're ready and I'll drive you." He turned to walk out the door.

"Pop, I'm sorry about all of this. I really am." He turned and looked at his father.

"Yeah, son, me too." Jim offered a smile then left the room.

CHAPTER 16

*L*exi parked her car at the local chicken restaurant in town. She saw Abby's car and knew she was inside already. She pulled out her phone and looked at the message again.

Lexi, before you hear anything, let me first say I'm so sorry. I love you and you're my friend. Blaine coming back was orchestrated through both me and him. He wanted you back. He was pissed you dumped him. He didn't want to let you go. You know how much of a control freak he is! Lexi, what I'm trying to say is, Blaine and I fucked at the party. We also slept together while y'all were still dating, before he took off with his band and before the band even made it big. Please believe me when I tell you I'm so sorry. I'm a selfish bitch and I don't deserve your friendship. I won't blame you if you hate me. Please, just know that Bobby Ray left because of me. I told him it was you who was with Blaine in the bathroom. He left because of me. I'm so sorry. If I could take it all back, I would in a heartbeat.

Lexi pocketed her phone again and pulled down the vanity mirror. She wiped the tears from her eyes again. Her heart ached for Bobby Ray. She wanted him back and she had to find a way to get to him. Her heart also ached because one of her best friends…, who she thought was a friend, had completely deceived her. She had no intentions of acting like a lady with what she was about to do. Her mama would say "do what you feel is right and do it with dignity." Her daddy would have said, "I'll get your mama to hold her down while you beat the shit outta her." She couldn't help but smile. She felt she'd be putting both sets of advice together in a few minutes.

She gathered her hair and pulled it back into a hair band. She smoothed her hands over her head then with a smirk in the mirror, she closed the vanity and got out of her car. The breeze in the air felt stale, almost like the environment was waiting to blow up around her. In just a few minutes, it would.

The host opened the restaurant door and welcomed her inside. She stalked past him then muttered, "I'm *beating* someone here."

"Pardon, ma'am?" He asked with alarm.

"Never mind, I see her," she growled. Lexi walked over to where Abby sat at a square table.

She stood up and offered a smile. "Lexi, you came!" She began to approach her friend when Lexi dropped her purse.

"How could you!" She pulled her fist back and landed it in Abby's nose, breaking it with a loud crack. Abby dropped to the ground and held her face while she screamed. "How could you! You fucked my boyfriend during school, you fucked him before he left then fucked him at the party and told my current boyfriend that it was ME?! Who the hell does that?"

A few of the patrons gasped and watched them. Someone mumbled '*whore*'.

"That's right; she's nothing but a damn whore!" Lexi kicked her in the leg and Abby cried out again.

"But I told you! I didn't have to and I did!" She continued to hold her nose. Abby momentarily pulled her hands back then freaked when she saw the amount of blood present in her hands.

"Oh, so you're the Good Samaritan now because you told me.

Oh, nice. Be glad I don't have a sister or brother. They'd want in on this, too. Never come to my house again. You are DEAD to me!" Lexi turned to leave then stopped by the ordering counter where the manager stood, shocked. "I apologize for what just took place. The whore bleeding down there will be happy to buy everyone's meals tonight. And if anything was damaged, she'll be happy to pay the bill for that, too." She turned to leave then stopped. "Thank you," she looked at the manager, "for not calling the police. I apologize for my part, but not for what I did."

The manager looked between Lexi and Abby then settled his gaze back on Lexi. "No ma'am. You had every right. If she really did those things, she deserved what she got. Now, go on before someone else calls the police." The manager shooed her out and she nodded with gratitude.

After Lexi was back outside, the events hit her like a wall. She gasped for air and tried to calm her heart. She felt like she would be sick when she realized she had been betrayed through her entire relationship with Blaine, Abby had never been her friend, and Bobby Ray had been caught in the middle. "FUCK YOU, BLAINE AND ABBY!"

Lexi got in her car and started it up, the adrenaline still pumping through her body. She heard her phone chime then it vibrated against her hip. She hoped it would be Bobby Ray, but at this point, she knew better.

Her mother's name came across the screen with a text of *call home now.*

She pressed dial and brought the phone up to her ear.

"*L*exi? Where are you?" Her mother's alarmed voice sounded through the line.

"Mama, I'm fine. If someone called you about Abby…"

Her mother cut her off. "Stop talking! Something's happened to Blaine."

"Honestly, Mama, I couldn't give a shit." She put the car into gear and started to take off when her mother spoke the next set of words into the phone.

"Honey, he overdosed last night and he's in the hospital. People have been calling here to tell you."

"He what?" She whispered. Everything in her hated Blaine for what he had done to her, but he didn't deserve to die. "What hospital?"

"Harris," she told her. "Now, hurry girl. Get on down there. I'll take care of things here. Just go."

"Yes, ma'am. Please, Mama, call his parents. Their number is in the phonebook by the coffee maker." Lexi hung up before her mother could answer. She pulled to the light and made a U-turn back toward downtown Fort Worth.

While the light was red, she stared at her phone for a moment. She sighed and rolled her eyes. "Not that she even deserves to know, or maybe I'm glutton for punishment..." Lexi sent a message to Abby, letting her know what happened to Blaine and what hospital he was in.

She tossed her phone in the seat and took off through the light when it turned green.

~

*M*akayla tried calling Bobby Ray again, and again, got his voicemail. "Dammit you idiot, take my damn call! There's some important shit I need to tell you that I DON'T want to say over voice mail!" She pressed end on her phone and tossed it into her purse. She groaned and laid her head back on the car seat.

Conner reached over and took her hand. "You're doing the best you can under the circumstances. Someone he'll talk to needs to call him. How about going to visit your uncle and have him call?"

"What, bribe Uncle Jim to do my dirty work? I never would have thought to do that." Her tone sarcastic she rolled her eyes.

"I'm trying here, baby. I just thought…"

"Well, I'm not going there. I don't want to resort to having my uncle call his son to relay a message that Abby is a lying whore and to get his ass back here. Oh and that Blaine overdosed and tried to kill himself. I'm sure that'll go over REAL well with them. They would shut the door in my face and not want to get their son involved in any of this shit."

"Alright, if you really feel that's what would happen, I won't say anymore." He squeezed her hand then let it go. Conner looked out the window toward Lexi's house. The trees blew gently in the breeze and he sighed. "Go on in, I'll come back for you later."

Makayla looked over at her boyfriend and gave him a sad look. "I'm sorry; I don't mean to be so shitty toward you. I'm just trying to be here for my best friend and get my cousin back."

"I know. It's fine. I love you. Call me when you're ready." He leaned in and kissed her.

"You're amazing, you know that?" She smiled and kissed him again.

"Only because you make me a better person."

She smiled again. "Don't you forget it," she teased him then winked. Makayla walked up to the house and knocked. Lexi's mother answered the door and let her inside.

She opened Lexi's bedroom door and found her lying in bed, facing the wall. "Go away." She pulled the covers up over her head.

"Thank you, Mrs. Griffin. I have it from here," Makayla smiled at her then turned toward Lexi. "No way, heifer. Scoot over, I'm climbing in."

Lexi pulled the covers down and looked over at her. Her face immediately changed from anger to sadness then she began to cry. "Oh Makayla!" She began to sob and her best friend went to her side, got under the covers with her, and held her tight.

"Shh, it's okay, it'll be okay." She ran her hand down her hair and hugged her friend.

"How could she? How could he? What did I do to deserve this? I want Robert; no, I need him back. Please?" She looked up at Makayla with a plea in her eyes. "Please, I need him!"

"I'm trying, honey, he's not taking my calls. Trust me; I'm trying. Conner thinks I should go talk to his parents and tell them what happened. I told him no way, that they'd slam the door in my face."

Lexi watched her for a moment as a moment of clarity hit her. She sat up suddenly and looked around her room.

"Whoa girl, you need to brush your hair." Makayla giggled and touched the rats nest in Lexi's hair.

"Leave my hair alone!" Lexi slapped her hand away. "He's right."

"Umm, who's right?" Makayla sat up next to her. "Lexi?"

"Conner! I need to go talk to his parents. They'd listen to me! They liked me!" She began to climb over Makayla.

"Ouch! Hey, what are you gonna do? Go over looking like a bum? Go take a shower and clean up. I'm gonna warn you now, honey, this is NOT a good idea."

"Why not?" Lexi turned on her. "I'll explain to them what happened and show them the text from Abby. They'll believe me and then they'll call Bobby Ray and tell him I didn't do anything!" She skipped toward her bathroom feeling a renewed sense of energy. "I mean, if anything, I could take some time off of work and…"

"Lexi, stop." Makayla took her hands and turned her around. "You heard what Blaine said. Your mother is losing the house. If you leave her here, she may need you if they come."

She nodded and the renewed energy left her. "I hadn't thought of that. Shit." Her happiness quickly faded. "You really think Blaine would do that? I mean, he's sort of incoherent right now."

"But… there's always a chance he did make that call. Who

knows though? Assuming my uncle makes that call and they tell him, Bobby Ray may come back here for you. Fall semester hasn't started quite yet."

"Oh, well now, I think that's just wishful thinking." She let go of her hands and walked into her bathroom. Lexi looked in the mirror then flinched. "Holy shit! Damn, look at me!" She laughed and shook her head. "Damn, you need to take a picture of this shit." She turned back to Makayla. "No, don't. You do it, I'll destroy your phone."

"Umm... bi-polar much? Get in the damn shower, woman. I'll go call my uncle and see if he'll sit down with me. I won't mention you just in case they say no. Okay?"

Lexi nodded and sighed. She needed to accept this might be it, that it might be over. And she needed to move forward, again. "Alright. I'll be ready in about thirty minutes." She then turned on the shower and shut the door.

CHAPTER 17

*L*exi followed Makayla outside and got into her car. Lexi leaned into the passenger seat and sighed. "The right thing to do would be to go see Blaine. I went by the day I found out but he was in a drug-induced coma or something like that. He had no idea I came by. It didn't even look like him."

"Yeah, you could go say your final 'leave me the hell alone' good-bye." She pulled out of the driveway and headed toward town. "Is that what you want to do first?"

"As much as I don't ever want to see him again, yes, only because it's the right thing to do."

A while later, they pulled into the hospital parking lot then walked inside. The smell of antiseptic tickled their noses and Lexi frowned. She hated hospitals. After asking the nurses station where to find Blaine, they took the elevator up to the fourth floor... Rehab on one side, suicide watch on the other.

They stepped out of the elevator and Lexi reached for Makayla's hand. "Don't leave me."

"I'm right here, honey." She squeezed Lexi's hand.

The floor was busy with nurses walking the floor and security surrounding what they assumed to be Blaine's door. The news media had not broken the story yet and they were happy not to have to fight to get around them.

Lexi checked in with the nurse at the station. "I'm Lexi Griffin. Blaine is... well he's my ex-boyfriend. I heard what happened and wanted to check on him."

The nurse nodded and allowed her to enter the room. "He's been asleep for a while. He's mumbled your name a few times."

Lexi's eyes widened. "What?"

"Maybe he'll talk to you if he's awake. The guards will be right outside. Please try not to make a disturbance." The nurse turned to leave her at the door.

Lexi turned to Makayla. "You're coming inside with me."

"Okay."

They stepped inside his room and tapped softly on the door. There wasn't an answer. Lexi looked at her friend and Makayla shrugged. She pushed on the door and peeked inside.

The room was dark except for a lamp in the corner of the room. Lexi found Blaine's mother asleep in the chair. She looked like she was uncomfortable, slumped over like that, and mascara was gathered under her eyes from crying. Her grayed hair was disheveled. In all the time she had known Blaine's mother, she had never seen the woman leave home without her hair done and make-up on her face.

Lexi stepped inside and she saw him. She wasn't ready for what was before her and she gasped. She quickly covered her lips and looked at his mother who had barely moved in the chair. Lexi looked back at Blaine and didn't recognize him.

His face was bruised as if he had been beaten up. He had tubes coming out of his nose, an IV giving him fluids, and monitors beeping throughout the room. Lexi shook her head and Makayla stepped in close behind her.

She held her best friend and whispered in her ear, "What the hell happened?"

Lexi shook her head, not having an answer.

"Excuse me, what the hell are you doing here?" Blaine's mother had woken up. Lexi looked over at her as she gave the girls stern, go-to-hell looks.

"Do you know the victim, ma'am?" A voice came in from behind him and Lexi turned.

The woman behind her was tall and in a gray business suit, holding a microphone. Suddenly a camera light flashed in her face and Lexi froze.

"Do you know the victim? Do you know Blaine? Are you a friend of his?" The reporter asked.

"Umm," is all Lexi got out.

"No, she doesn't know him. Not anymore!" Blaine's mother came up behind them and started to push everyone out of the room. "This whore screwed my son over so badly he tried to take his life because of her!"

"Excuse me?" Lexi quickly turned around and glared at his mother. "I did no such thing! You obviously heard the wrong story!"

"Oh no, I've seen enough of this shit and of you... you whore!"

The reporter was eating this up. She pushed herself further into the room. Makayla began to run interference. She shook her head and got between Lexi, the mother, and the reporter, pushing the reporter out of the room. "Give them space. He's been in a severe trauma. Have a little respect."

"But it's our right to get the story!" the reporter told her.

"And it's my right to say no comment. Now get out." Makayla pushed her out of the room and closed the door. She turned back and found Lexi staring down Blaine's mother. "Alright, now you two need to calm down. Blaine didn't get screwed over by Lexi. Blaine cheated on her then manipulated her something fierce a few days ago." Makayla went through the story of what happened between Blaine, Abby, and Lexi.

Lexi stepped away from the mother and leaned against the wall, wrapping her arms around her body. "I only wanted to come see how he was, and hopefully, get some closure between us. It's time we both had it."

"Whatever, I don't buy any of this nonsense!" his mother yelled out. "Say your good-byes and get the hell out!"

Blaine groaned and his heart monitor sped up slightly. Lexi, Makayla, and Blaine's mother all shifted their attention on him.

Lexi looked at his mother for a moment then stepped closer toward his bedside. She took a seat in the chair next to the bed then took his hand. "Blaine, as much as I feel sorry for you right now, every bit of me hates you for what you did." She looked up to his eyes and found him watching her. "Oh, you're awake?"

His mother nodded while she stood on the other side of the bed. "He's been in and out of consciousness."

"Oh," she muttered. Lexi looked back at him again and swallowed hard. "I don't know why you thought it was okay to do what you did, but you have people here that love you. You can't hurt yourself like this and think all will be okay in the morning. If you have an addiction problem…"

"The lab results came back with coke and ecstasy," his mother told her.

"I had no idea he was even using." Lexi looked at Makayla and she shook her head no. "Do his bandmates know?"

His mother nodded. "I was able to get in touch with them through his manager. They're covering the PR for it, or as much as they can." She nodded toward the door then sighed. "If you're done, I'd appreciate you leaving now. I think you've caused enough trouble for one day."

Lexi stared at her for a moment. "You need to realize I didn't do this. I didn't make him do this and I didn't make him give me an ultimatum to stay with him or he'll take ownership of my family's farm."

"Whatever," she mumbled.

She knew she wouldn't get anywhere so she rolled her eyes and looked back at Blaine. "You and I are through. There will never be a me and you, ever again. You will not contact me, you will not follow me anywhere, and you sure as hell won't be taking my family's farm. Good-bye, Blaine. I only wish I could get all those years back. Sadly, I can't." She stood and let go of his hand. "Don't bother trying to find me to apologize. I'm sure I've made myself clear, but just in case, I've already spoken to an attorney to protect our assets until my mother can get our affairs in order."

Blaine closed his eyes and a single tear slid into his hairline. Lexi took a deep breath then turned away from him. She walked out of the room and out of his life. Closing the room door behind her, she let out the long, deep breath she'd been holding then broke down into tears.

Makayla instantly pulled her into a hug. "Come on; let's get out of here before the evil reporter comes back." As if her words were calling her, the woman came around the corner.

"Please! Talk to us!" The reporter came running down the hall just as Makayla hit the elevator door button. They stepped inside and the doors shut just as the reporter reached it.

"Get me home, please. I feel like I'm going to be sick." Lexi leaned against the wall and used the palms of her hands to wipe her face. She sniffed and looked at Makayla. "His mother is a wretched bitch!"

"Umm, you think?" Makayla snickered and Lexi smiled. "He'll recover you know. He'll be fine."

Lexi nodded. The elevator opened, they stepped out, made their way to Makayla's car, and headed back toward home.

~

*R*obert sat slumped in a chair in the guest bedroom of his mother and stepfather's house. He stared out the window and watched the leaves blow against the trees. He yawned and then looked at his phone when it rang. He saw his father's number light up and he decided to answer. "Hey Pop. How you doing?" His voice was monotone and flat.

"Hey, son. You sound like you're about to fall asleep. Did I catch you at a bad time?"

He leaned forward and held his forehead in his hand. He sighed, but didn't say anything.

"Robert? Are you there son?"

"Yeah, Pop, I'm here." He hesitated for a moment then sobbed once. "Pop, I can't get her out of my head. I love her, even after what happened, after what she did, I still love her. It fucking hurts!" He sobbed once more, sat up and wiped his eyes, and shook it off. "I'm fine, I'm fine. I'm sure this isn't why you called."

"Actually, it is. I'm not sure if you've heard or not, but there's been some... developments."

"What do you mean?" Robert stood up from his chair and turned toward his computer, clicking the mouse. The screen came to life. "What's up?"

"Seems that kid, Blaine, overdosed the other night and tried to kill himself."

"Seriously?" Robert keyed in a few keystrokes and sure enough, the local newspaper in Fort Worth had the story covered. He read the head line and looked at the picture captured of him. He shook his head. "Damn, he looks like shit."

"There's more," his father said. "Lexi came by and filled us in."

"What the hell did she have to say?" His voice was cold and harsh.

"Now you need to listen to me, son; can you do that?" Robert didn't say anything. "Good." His father went into the details about Abby and Blaine, what they did, how they sabotaged him and Lexi and how Abby had come clean about it. "Oh and son, you'll be happy to know that Lexi gave that Abby girl a good old country ass whoopin'. You'd have been proud of her." He chuckled into the phone.

Robert sighed and leaned forward on the desk, holding his head. "I'm a damned fool!"

"Son, she understands, now, why you left. She knows your heart was broken before and that Abby was her friend. You had no reason to doubt her."

"Actually, I did. She tried to come onto me after she told me about Lexi and Blaine."

"And she also came clean about that, too."

"Damn, so did Lexi whoop her ass good then, huh?" Robert chuckled. "Shit! I need to get back there! Pop! Can I…"

"Son, your room is still here for you. Get yourself on the next flight. If you're serious about moving here for her, then you need to talk to your Dean about transferring."

"Yes, sir. It's the weekend; no one is there. But Monday morning, I'll start making the calls."

"Oh son, there's one more thing." His father went into how Lexi's mother was about to lose her farm due to foreclosure and how Blaine threatened to take it away from them. "She voiced concern just because he's gone doesn't mean he's out. She needs to find a way to pay off the mortgage or at least, get it caught up."

"Shit, are you serious? I didn't realize it was to that point. Alright, I'll take care of that. Please, no one knows I'm coming back, okay?"

"You bet, son. I love you. See you soon."

"Thank you for calling, Pop."

"Well, thank you for finally answering." He chuckled then hung up.

Robert set down his phone and ran down into the living room. "Mom? Dad? You down here? I need to talk and need a huge favor!"

CHAPTER 18

*A*bout two weeks had passed since Lexi had said her final good-bye to Blaine. He left the hospital and voluntarily checked himself into rehab. He made national news when he did. "You know you've made it big when you go to rehab and everyone's talking about it," Makayla told her the other night over dinner. "Looks like they may be replacing him in the band, too."

Lexi leaned against the counter at the tack store and stared off into her own world. She missed Bobby Ray. Missed his touch, his scent, his kissing her, the way he held her, looked at her, and loved her. She quickly swiped a tear away when a young woman approached the counter.

She heaved up a bag of treats for horses and smiled at Lexi. "It's a beautiful day. Whatever's wrong honey, go outside and run around a little. Let the sun warm your spirits."

A smile formed on Lexi's lips, but it didn't reach her eyes. "Yes ma'am." She gave her the total then offered to help her carry the heavy bag out to her truck.

"Whoever broke your heart honey, he's not worth your tears. You deserve someone who will treat you like you a princess." The woman patted Lexi on her arm, then handed her a few dollars as a tip.

"Tipping isn't necessary, but thank you." She smiled again then closed up the tail gate. "Enjoy your afternoon and thank you for coming in." Lexi turned and walked back into the tack store. She saw her manager walking toward her. "Hey Joe, I'm going in the back for a while. Call me if you need me on the floor."

"Lexi," Joe, her manager called to her. "Cheer up, would ya? You're depressing the shit outta me." He chuckled and walked behind the counter.

She rolled her eyes, walked into the back, and shut the door behind her. A long sigh left her lips and she sat down on top of a few feedbags that been set up. Her elbows pressed into her thighs and her head fell between her hands. Lexi began to sob again and her shoulders shook. "Maybe I should have fought harder? Maybe I should have flown to Georgia and confronted him? Hell, maybe I can get Abby to tell him what happened." She thought about that last statement for a moment and anger rose inside of her. "If I ever see that whore again..."

"You'll do what, exactly? Kick her ass? Well honey, get in line." Makayla shut the door behind her and approached her best friend.

Lexi turned around and watched her friend approach. The sobs came again and she cried. "I already beat her ass." She sobbed once more. "Please, tell me you talked to him?"

Makayla sat down on her knees in front of her friend then pulled her into an embrace. "Yeah, I know you did. And rightfully so." She shook her head. "No honey, I haven't talk to him yet. I'm sorry." She felt Lexi's body shake as she cried. "But I know someone who has."

"What?" She pulled back and wiped her face with her palms. She sniffed and stared at her friend. "Who? What did he say?" She hoped he knew she hadn't cheated on him, that it was all Abby and Blaine.

"You really need to clean your face. You have mascara down your..."

"MAKAYLA!" Lexi yelled. "Who did he talk to?"

"Geez woman!" She smiled and wiped away one of Lexi's tears. "My uncle called him, Bobby Ray's daddy. He talked to him."

"Okay..." Lexi sat and waited, then raised her hands. "And?"

"And... well I think you need to go home. Your mama needs you. Something's happened."

"Wait, what? You said Jim called Bobby Ray and now I need to get home to my mom? Is she okay? Did something happen?"

Makayla laughed. "I hate being cryptic, but trust me, you need to get home. Your mama is just fine."

Lexi stood and kept her eyes on her friends. "You better not be messing with me, Makayla. I can't take anymore shit from anyone. Blaine leaving and cheating with who the hell else knows, meeting and losing Bobby Ray, then Blaine coming back and threatening to take our farm? Yeah, too much."

"I can't claim to understand, because I don't. All I can say is get your damn ass home!" Makayla smiled then pulled Lexi into a hug. "Now go. I already told Joe you're going home."

"You did?" She pulled away looking a little surprised. "Wow, thank you." She wiped her tears and looked at her fingers. "Yeah, you weren't kidding about the mascara." She looked up and laughed a little. "Umm, Makayla?"

"Yeah, honey?" She smiled.

"What am I walking into when I get home?" She felt her heart pick up and her stomach turn nervous. If this continued, she knew she would be sick all over the floor.

"I can't tell you, just get home. That's all I'm saying. I love you, honey, but you need to go!" Makayla grabbed her shoulders and turned her around, then pushed her out of the tack inventory room. "Go!"

"Fine! I'm going!" She shook her head and looked back at her friend with a smile then went to the counter where she hid her purse. She pulled it out and took off toward the door.

"Good luck, girl," Joe called after her.

"See ya later, Joe. Thanks again!" She walked out the door and shaded her eyes when the sunlight hit her. Lexi pulled her keys out and unlocked her car. She shut the door and sat there in the heat of the afternoon. The sound in the car was completely void of anything and she could hear a ringing in her ears. She sighed and stared at her dashboard. "Lord, please help me." She started up her car and put it into gear, then pulled out of the parking lot.

~

*A*fter picking up his son from the airport, Jim headed toward Mrs. Griffin's home. "You have everything you need?"

"Yes, sir. It's all here. Rick was great in securing everything and getting it all set up. Mrs. Griffin was completely stunned, grateful, and I think she cried a little over the phone." He chuckled. "I know she's happy with how things have turned out."

"I would hope so. Rick is a good man. I'm glad he's been there for you. Your mother is lucky to have him."

"Hell, yeah she is!" Robert laughed. "He's done a lot of good for a lot of people. Sometimes she acts like she's into it, but I know she's not. She would much rather be at her garden club than serving the community. She has a good poker face, I'll give her that."

"Well, I don't care to talk about your mother, so let's not."

"Fair enough." Robert sat there for a moment, holding the contract in his hands from Rick. "Does Lexi know?" He looked over his to father.

"Not that I'm aware of. I called Makayla and told her to send her home, but that's all I told her."

"She has no idea?" Robert asked curiously.

"Oh no, but I think she suspects." He grinned. "I did tell her I talked to you and I know she told Lexi that much."

"Yeah about that. I'm sorry I didn't take anyone's calls. I just couldn't deal with anymore lies."

"You realize the only one who lied was that one girl, Annie, Arlene, hell, I don't remember her name."

Robert chuckled. "Abby?"

"Yeah, that's her. She and that Blaine are the only ones who lied. Now he's in rehab, or so the news tells us, and she's... well I don't know where she is. Don't care really."

"Yeah, neither do I." Robert didn't say anything else. He watched the farm land as they drove by, fields and fields of corn and wheat up for the harvest. "Pop?"

"Yeah, son?" Jim looked to his son, then back to the road.

"Did you think Sabrina was worth this much effort?" He looked to his father.

"Not at first, but she knew I was. It just took me a while to see it. She's a wonderful woman, son. She helped me when your mother left and now she's all I think about. What is Lexi to you? Is she worth fighting for? Is she worth relocating yourself and starting over?"

Robert sat back in his seat and thought about his answer for a few minutes. "Pop, before all the crap with Blaine went down, I would have followed her to the ends of the earth."

"And after the lies? She wasn't worth fighting for?"

"Not when I thought she wanted him back. There's no way I can compete with that."

"Why not?" Jim pulled off the main road and turned down a dirt road headed toward Lexi's farmhouse.

"He was her first love." Robert looked down at his hands. "He had a life time with her. I've had like, five minutes."

"I understand, but son, would she have fought for you?"

Robert shrugged. "Honestly, I don't know."

"Are you sure about that?"

He shook his head. "Honestly, if she thought Abby had come on to me, she would have kicked her ass." He chuckled then his own words sunk in. "Ahh hell, Pop. She did kick her ass because Abby tried coming on to me. I'm such a jackass!"

Jim chuckled. "No son, you're stubborn and thick headed, just like me. Look at it this way." He pulled up to the farmhouse and put the truck into park. "You have all the time in the world to make it up to her. Now, if you're ready, let's go inside."

Robert nodded with a smile. He looked back down at the envelope containing the contract Mrs. Griffin had discussed with Rick then sighed. "Let's do this."

CHAPTER 19

*L*exi pulled up to her farmhouse and stared at Mr. Shaw's truck in the driveway. Her heart beat rapidly in her chest and the butterflies continued to flip in her stomach. "Dammit, Lexi, calm the hell down!"

She sighed, opened the door, and stepped out. She gently closed it in hopes of not drawing attention to the fact that she was home. She looked around the area but didn't see anything out of place or order. "What's going on?" She whispered to herself.

Suddenly, the front door opened to the laughter of her mother. "Thank you so much Robert! Please, tell Mr. McAlister he will not be sorry!" She pulled Robert into a hug.

Lexi stood there slack jawed. Was she hallucinating? Was that really Bobby Ray her mother was hugging? He let go of her mother and Mr. Shaw stepped out with them and stood on the porch.

"You're very welcome. Homestead law is in place for a reason. He's anxious to get started in business with you. Trust me, he couldn't be happier." He handed her a few pieces of paper, then hugged the woman again.

His father tapped Robert on the shoulder. When he turned around, he motioned toward Lexi. "Son?"

Their eyes met and both stood in their place for what felt like forever: neither moving, neither speaking.

"Mrs. Griffin, if I may escort you out for coffee with my new bride to celebrate?"

"Oh, Mr. Shaw, that sounds lovely. Let me grab my purse."

A moment later, Lexi's mother and Robert's father walked past him then her mother stopped by Lexi with a smile. "Give'em hell, baby. He's done well for us." She smiled and looked up at Robert on the steps. "And close your mouth. You look like you're catching flies!"

Lexi was the first to break eye contact and she glared at her mother. "Really, Mama?" She shook her head then looked back at Robert.

"Right, that's our cue, Mr. Shaw. Shall we?"

Jim grinned at Lexi and Robert then nodded at Mrs. Griffin. "Have a great afternoon." He got in his Dually and left the house. He knew Robert would find a way home... eventually.

Mrs. Griffin smiled getting into her car and pulled out of the long driveway, leaving a trail of dust in her wake.

Robert pressed his palms against the railing and leaned into it. "You look beautiful. Lexi, I'm so..."

"Why the hell did you not take my calls?" She stared at him for a moment then shook her head. "You can't just come here and tell me I look beautiful and pretend like the last few weeks didn't happen!"

Robert flinched at her words. He came down the stairs from the porch and walked up to her. "I came back here for you." His words were soft and gentle.

"No!" She turned her back to him and shook her head. "You thought I did the unspeakable and wouldn't even consider hearing my side of what didn't happen!" She started walking, needing to put distance between them. *Ironic*, she thought, *how much she*

wanted to see him and now she can't get enough space between them.
She stopped in front of an old tractor wheel that her father had
buried half into the ground years ago. Her father planned to build
a garden for her mother around it, thinking this was a beautiful
place to start one, and a beautiful wheel would complement it.

"Lexi, dammit! Stop!" He jogged to catch up to her. He grabbed
her arms and turned her around. "Shit, don't cry."

"Why the hell not? All I've been doing is crying! You left me,
Robert; you left me! No, you left us! As much as you told me
you're not Blaine in all of this, you were quick as hell to compare
me to your ex!"

He shook his head and covered his mouth with his hand. He
adjusted the weight on his feet then placed his hands on his hips.
"I know saying I'm sorry will never be enough, but please, I'm
sorry."

"For which part exactly? For believing that whore's lie or for
not having enough faith in me not to fuck Blaine?" She turned her
back on him again, but this time, rather than running off, she
stayed still. "I can't believe you thought I would do that."

"I know, and I'll always be sorry for that, but for a second, try
to see things from my point of view. Your *friend*," he put emphasis
on the word friend, "told me she found you two in the bathroom
getting it on. Blaine was your first love and you two had just
broken up. He came to town and we went to the party you wanted
to go to. I didn't want to go because I was concerned that you
seeing him would ignite old feelings. I watched him put his arms
around you. I had convinced myself I was right to the point I
wouldn't take anyone's call."

"I'm trying, but honestly, it's hard for me to even think about
being with Blaine after all the shit he put me through." She turned
around to face him and was taken by surprise at the tears in his
eyes. The hardness in her heart softened a little. "Do you know he
threatened to take our farm if I didn't go back to him? He had just
slept with Abby and came to tell me that. Then when he tried to

put his arms around me, you must have turned right when I pushed him off and he grabbed me by the throat. A guy I never met before threw him off of me then according to a few people at the party, Abby threatened him with her shot gun."

"He did what?" Anger rose inside of Robert and he shook his head. "Mother fucker," he mumbled. "Lexi, dammit I'm so sorry. No man, no matter what, should ever touch a woman like that." He lowered his gaze and his head dropped between his shoulders.

"I also heard about him threatening to take everything you had. That's one of the reason's I'm came back." He lifted his gaze to hers and chanced it by stepping closer. "My dad told me everything." He reached up and brushed stray hairs behind her ear.

"You came back because of our farm dilemma?" She broke eye contact and lowered her gaze and head.

"I told you that's one of the reason's I came back." He lifted her chin. "You're the other. I love you, Lexi. I don't want to be without you again. I can't go on in life if you're not there with me. You are everything in this world I need."

She began to sob again. "Robert..." She cupped her face and cried into her hands.

"Shh, baby, it's okay." He wrapped his arms around her slender frame and held onto her. "I love you so much." He kissed the top of her head. "I hope you find it in your heart to forgive me. I'll work every day of my life, making this up to you."

She sniffed and pulled her hands away long enough to wipe the tears from her face. "You love me?" She hiccupped and her lips pulled in a faint smile. He smiled and nodded a few times. "You came back for me and you know the truth. That's all I ever wanted." She leaned her face toward his chest, her forehead resting against his chin. She inhaled his scent and closed her eyes. His cologne invaded her senses and she felt, for the first time in a few weeks, at peace. He had come home for her. She felt the corners of her lips pull into a smile. "I love you, too, Bobby Ray."

"Always with the Bobby Ray," he teased. He lifted her chin

again and looked into her eyes. "I love you, Lexi. I'm here to stay. I've put in the transfer and I'm moving. I won't be too far away."

"What? Are you serious?" Her voice went up an octave and she smiled wide. "You're not going back to Georgia?"

"Nope. Afraid you're stuck with me." He grinned and kissed her forehead.

"No, I'm afraid you're stuck with me." She laughed and sniffed once more. "Oh, I'm so done with crying. Kiss me."

"Yes ma'am." He cupped her face and crushed his lips to hers. Lexi's fingers tightened in his shirt as she tried pulling him closer to her. His hands moved down her arms to her legs. He lifted her and sat her down on the tractor wheel, then wrapped her legs around his waist. "Damn, I missed you, woman."

"Oh baby, I missed you so much." She had her arms around his neck and her fingers moved in his hair, tugging it slightly.

His hands moved up her thighs then around her backside, cupping her bottom. He gently pulled her closer until her hips were pressed against his.

Their kissing became more heated and when she whimpered against his lips, Robert felt himself losing control. "I need you," he growled.

"Well, I'll race you to the house, then. First one there wins bragging rights on the shower."

"Then you'd better get your ass running!" He reluctantly stepped back and pulled her down to the ground. "Ready? One..."

"THREE!" Lexi laughed and took off running. She looked back at him and loved the smile on his lips.

"Oh, I'm getting you for that!" He yelled and took off running. He could easily beat her, he knew it, but decided to have a little fun instead. He made grabby hands at her ass and she laughed even louder.

"Oh my god, stop it! I'll fall!"

"Then I'll catch you!" He insisted.

They made it to the porch and Lexi reached for the screen

door and threw it open. Robert came up behind her and walked inside. As soon as she shut the front door, he took her body and pressed her against the wall. He lifted her hands above her head and held them with one hand, the other moving down her slender arm to her breasts.

She gasped against his lips and fought to keep kissing him, even when he pulled away. "I need you," she whispered.

"You'll get me soon, baby." He kissed down her neck, then nibbled on her hear. "You're so damn sexy."

She tugged at her hands and groaned. "I want to touch you."

"Not yet." He grinned against her skin then moved her legs apart with his knee. He pressed his pelvis against her and she moaned softly. "Fuck, I need you just as bad." He finally let go of her hands to grab her shirt and yank it over her head. He took in the sight of her breasts and groaned, then ran his lips across her bust line.

She gasped and her fingers moved to his hair, gripping it. She pulled him closer and her head tilted back against the wall.

His hands kneaded her breasts and he felt her hardened nipples against his palms. Robert's lips moved down over her bra and he lightly bit the erect bud.

She writhed and her lips parted. She looked to him with lust in her eyes. "I need you," she begged, "please!"

He growled against her breast then moved his lips back to hers and crushed them. He kissed her hard and lifted her body as her legs wrapped around his waist. He carried her toward her bedroom and kicked the door closed behind him.

They crashed into her bed and fell onto it. Lexi pulled at his shirt and tugged it over his head. "I need to feel your skin against mine!" She moved her hands to his jeans and fumbled with his buckle.

"I'll get this. You get naked." He smirked and stood up.

She laughed and removed her boots, unbuckled her belt and jeans, and pushed them down her legs.

Robert began removing one of his boots and tried to balance on the other foot. He began to topple over and jumped on his foot until he landed against her dresser.

Lexi laughed and sat up to watch him strip.

He chuckled and got the boot off then the other. He removed the rest of his clothes then he stared at her body for a moment and shook his head.

"What is it?" She asked with a little alarm.

"You're so damn beautiful." He sat on the edge of her bed and gently ran his fingers down between her breasts.

"Oh..." she gasped and closed her eyes to the sensation. He moved his fingers over her stomach and she smiled as she tried not to giggle.

Robert climbed onto the bed as Lexi watched him. He positioned himself in front of her then reached around to unfasten her bra. He gently pulled it down her arms then tossed it to the floor. He took in the sight of her full, luscious breasts. "Lay back down." After she lay back, he reached for her panties and gently pulled them down her body. He let them drop to the floor while his eyes never left her body. "So beautiful."

He moved himself over her body and looked down into her eyes. His length pressed against her entrance and he felt her moving against him, teasing him. "I love you, Lexi."

She smiled and ran her hands up his arms. His muscles moved against her touch as she held onto him. "I love you so much, Robert." She lifted her head up and he met her half way and kissed her.

He reached between them and lined himself up, then pushed inside her. He groaned against her lips as she gasped. "Baby, damn I missed you," he told her as he pulled back and thrust into her again.

"I love you," she whimpered and gripped his arms tighter. "I love you so much. Please, never leave me again."

"Never," he whispered against her lips.

CHAPTER 20

A few months had passed and winter break started up. Robert found himself thinking back to when he returned for Lexi and offered the contract his stepfather had drawn up for her mother.

He knew Lexi was The One long before the drama unfolded with Abby and Blaine, but like his father, he had been stubborn about it. When Lexi told him she had learned what Robert had done for her family, any thoughts of him leaving, their past, or anything to do with Blaine and Abby immediately left her mind. She knew he was The One, even before that gesture if she was being honest with herself.

Robert's stepfather, Rick, invested in Mrs. Griffin's farm and their agreement hired workers for her. He owned 49 percent of her farm while Mrs. Griffin retained ownership at 51 percent. As for payment, "Send me supplies of the vegetables and 10% of what you sell. Everything else is yours. I think we'll be family soon enough and family help each other out when needed."

Robert loved his stepfather for what he had been able to do. His mother hadn't quite understood the urgency of the matter but had gone along with it anyway. When Robert had shown the contract to Mrs. Griffin, she had immediately begun to cry. "I hope my daughter gets her shit together, son, because I want you to marry her!"

He recalled the memories while looking over engagement rings. He was graduating soon and Lexi had been able to start back into large animal veterinary school again. He wanted something perfect for her.

The female sales associate, maybe in her mid-forties, walked forward, and stopped in front of him. "What may I assist you with today?"

He smiled and asked about a few of the rings, their shapes, and if any represented anything different with the styles."

"Truth be told, it's what the bride fancies the most. What do you see her in, sir?" She pulled out a few of the more expensive rings and Robert's brows rose. *I wonder if she could even carry that on her finger?* He thought to himself. "Umm, maybe something not so... huge." He smiled to the sales woman.

She nodded and pulled a few trays of engagement rings. Robert looked them over then finally settled on a three different styles; princess cut, pear cut, and round cut. He was having a hard time deciding which of the three were more Lexi.

His phone vibrated in his pocket and when he saw the caller, he grinned. "Makayla. What are you doing right now?"

～

*C*lass had ended a little early today and before going home to Robert, she thought it would be nice to spend the afternoon with Makayla. She noticed a crowd of people, mainly girls, gathered around someone on a motorcycle. She assumed he was probably a male model or someone famous. Sometimes there was no telling around campus.

"Lexi?" The deep, familiar voice sounded and the women surrounding the man, turned to face her. He stood up from his bike and heavy, leather boots sounded on the ground as he approached her.

She swallowed hard, having never expected to see Blaine again, and especially not at her college. "What are you doing here?" She asked, her eyes wide with surprise and fright. The last time she had seen him he had overdosed and had been in the hospital. That seemed like ages ago.

Blaine had not only cleaned up, he had beefed up on his muscle tone as well. Maybe kicking one habit started another. A musical gym rat. Images of actors who were called, 'triple threats' entered her mind; men like *Hugh Jackman*.

Blaine smiled to her. "It's good to see you, too." He leaned forward to hug her, then corrected himself and cleared his throat. "I was hoping to see you, spend a little time with you this afternoon."

"What? Are you serious?" Her voice changed from surprised to irate. "After the stunt you pulled last time I saw you? You want to spend time with me?"

"Yes," he said matter-of-factly. "I want to apologize and tell you I was wrong, and I'm clean now, too."

"Good for you, I'm glad you're clean. I'm sure your mother is, too. I'm sorry, but I don't think I can forgive you, at least not yet. You really hurt me, Blaine. You deceived me and Robert. Then you had an on and off again fling with Abby. And let's not forget you threatened to take my farm. What the hell got into you?"

"Where do I start?" He rubbed his hand across the back of his neck. He turned when he felt someone tap his shoulder.

"Can we get your autograph?" The woman gave him pleading eyes. Blaine took her paper and when he wasn't looking, she looked at Lexi and sent daggers toward her.

Lexi found herself laughing. "Go to your fans. They want you more than I do."

"Oh, I'll take you to my house! It's just down..." the fan started.

"No," Blaine told the woman. He turned back to Lexi, "I need to do this. Please."

"I'll wait over here for you, if that's okay?" The woman called back.

Blaine ignored her and kept his attention on Lexi. He raised his brows while he started at her. "Well, that's a first," she told him and crossed her arms. "Okay, spill."

"Lexi," he sighed and rubbed his neck again.

She noticed a few new tattoos on his neck, arms, and he had a new lip ring. She shook her head and waited for him to start. "I have places to be. Hurry up."

"Wow, no love lost, huh?" He grinned and when she was about to walk away, "Stop, I'm sorry, it was my failed attempt at a joke. Alright, you want to know? I was on coke, X, crack, meth, and acid. I smoked some weed laced with some shit that made me hallucinate. The night I OD'd, I snorted all the coke I had. It almost killed me." He kept his eyes on the ground as he continued. "I was checked into rehab, involuntarily, to get cleaned up. My manager told me I had to do this or I was out of the band." He looked up at her. "I'm two-hundred forty days sober. It's still hard as hell, but I'm doing it.

"With having a clean mind, I want to clean my conscience. I'm truly sorry for any harm I caused and for threatening you in any way. I never intended to follow through. Hell, I probably wouldn't have remembered in the first place. Just... Lexi, I'm very sorry. And if you find it in your heart to forgive me, I'd be forever grateful." He looked up at her and stepped closer. "I truly am sorry."

She watched him and took in his words. "My god, you were on a lot of shit. How did you get started? Or maybe I should ask why you got started?"

"I noticed after being on the road night after night, playing all the time, I was exhausted. Between the booze and the sex," he noticed Lexi cringe at this, "I was having a hard time keeping up. Someone offered me a line of coke and told me it would broaden my horizons in ways I would never expect. Damn, were they right! My energy level kicked up a notch and I felt like I could do anything, be anything!

"Eventually, coke lead to crack and that lead to meth. I don't even know when it started getting out of control. I just know that I have felt better these last few months than I have in years." He stepped closer to her again, closing the distance. He lowered his voice some and looked into her eyes. "Please, forgive me. I need your forgiveness."

Lexi bit her lip and wished Robert were here with her. She felt nervous being this close to Blaine. He was her first love, her first partner, her first everything. They had seen each other naked many times, but in this moment, this closeness made her feel uneasy. "Listen Blaine, I think it's best you leave. I'm getting ready to meet up with Makayla and later, with Bobby Ray."

He lowered his head and sighed. "So you're still seeing him after everything I did to fuck that up?" He looked back up at her again.

"Yes. Matter of fact, we live together now and I'm positive he'll be asking me to marry him soon. So, again, I think it's best you leave."

He nodded and took a small step back. "I didn't come here to try to win you back or anything like that. I know my time with you is over. I just need your forgiveness so I can close this shit and move on myself." He turned and headed back to his motorcycle and the women surrounding it suddenly came alive.

She sighed and shook her head. "I'm such a glutton for punishment." She called out to him, "Blaine, wait."

He turned and walked back to her. "Yeah?"

"Come here." She closed the distance and pulled him into a hug. "All is forgiven."

His arms wrapped around her and he squeezed her. "Thank you. You have no idea what that means to me."

"Oh, I'm not done." She pulled away and removed his arms

from her body. "There's a few more people you should apologize to. You realize that, right?"

He nodded, "Yeah," then lowered his gaze. "Where are they?"

~

$\mathcal{R}$obert pulled into his driveway and found someone on a motorcycle waiting in his driveway. He got out of his truck and approached the man in leather. "Something I can help you with?" When the stranger's head raised up to meet his gaze, Robert stopped walking. "Blaine? What the hell are you doing here?" He felt adrenaline shoot through his body.

"I didn't come here to fight. I actually came here to apologize." He sighed. "As much as I hate to admit this to you, of all people, I fucked up. Royally."

Robert chuckled. "Yeah, you did."

Blaine shook his head. "My counselor wants me to come and apologize to those I hurt and wronged while I was high. Part of my rehab or some shit."

"Counselor? Wow, you're taking this rehab thing seriously. Good for you."

Blaine gritted his teeth. "Look, I fucked up shit with Lexi and I've accepted that. I've already spoken with her and..."

"Wait, you did? When?"

"Earlier today. She told me where I could find you. Why, is that a problem?" Blaine wanted to smirk knowing he put the thought of doubt in his head.

"No, not at all. Just surprised she sent you here. Y'all have a good talk then?"

Blaine dropped his smirk and replaced it with chagrin. "Yeah, we did. That's why I'm here. I'm sorry for how things went down. There's no excuse so I won't give you one."

"I appreciate that. Did she forgive you?"

"Yeah, I could tell she didn't want to, but this is Lexi we're talking about." Blaine smiled and looked down to the ground.

"Yeah, I know. She's a good woman and if she'll have me, I plan on marrying her."

Blaine looked up. "She deserves happiness. If she's found it with you, then I'm happy for her. And you, yeah you can suck my ass. But before you do the deed, I need your forgiveness."

Robert couldn't help but laugh. "You're unbelievable. You want my forgiveness then want me to suck your ass?" He shook his head and chuckled. "Get off my property before I shoot your ass. I forgive the act, Blaine, but I can't forgive you as a person. Now you need to leave my property." Robert stood taller and crossed his arms over his chest.

"Fine," Blaine rolled his eyes and kick started his bike. "Then suck my left nut." He flipped him off and spun his bike around, kicking up gravel toward Robert.

He stepped out of the way and shook his head. Blaine sped off down the road and the growl of his bike eventually faded. "What an asshole." Robert walked back toward his home and went inside, setting his carrier bags and the package from the jewelry store down. He pulled the white leather box from the bag and discarded the evidence. He shoved the small box into his pants pocket then walked into his bedroom to shower and get ready for what he knew would be an epic evening. The unexpected visit from Blaine was already far from his mind.

CHAPTER 21

$\mathcal{L}$exi headed home to her mother's house that evening. She had a suspicion that tonight would be the night Robert asked her to marry him and she wanted to be ready. She stood in her old bedroom closet, while her hair dripped from the shower she had just finished. She eyed the black dress Robert had seen her in that day at the dress shop, what felt like years ago.

She ran her hand over the soft, silky fabric and smiled. "He will lose his shit if I wear this. I wonder if he even remembers it."

"Well, honey, then I suggest you wear it and commence the shit losing."

Lexi laughed and turned to find her mother in her old bedroom. "Mama!"

Mrs. Griffin smiled. "Well? I want to see this dress that will make him lose his shit, as you said."

She shook her head and smiled, happy with how things had turned out for them. Robert flew in and rescued not only her, but also her family, when they needed it. He had never asked, he had never held it over her. He had done it because he loved her.

Lexi found herself smiling as she thought of him. She casually looked down at her left hand, imagining a perfect ring he would pick out for her hand to wear. She sighed then pulled the dress down from the closet. "Alright, Mama. You'll need to zip it up my back." She hung the dress on the frame of the closet door then walked over to her bed.

She pulled out a matching bra and panty set then turned to her mother. "Can you give me a minute to get dressed?"

"Child, I used to wipe your ass. Get naked." Mrs. Griffin rolled her eyes and walked toward the dress, then turned her back to Lexi.

"Mama!" She laughed and shook her head. She grabbed her panties and pulled them on under the towel. She glanced at her mother and, satisfied she wasn't looking, dropped her towel, and quickly put on her bra. "Ok, hand me the dress, please."

Her mother turned and pulled the dress off the hanger then unzipped it. Mrs. Griffin smiled a sweet smile, but it had something knowing to it, as if she knew a secret.

"Mama, what are you up to?" Lexi stepped into the dress and pulled it up. She turned around for her mother to zip her up.

"I have no idea what you mean, child." Her mother zipped up the dress then stepped back and took in her daughter. The halter style dress hugged her body in just the right places. "Wow honey, you look amazing. Yeah, he will definitely lose his shit when he sees you."

Lexi laughed then bit her lip. "Is that a good or bad thing, Mama?" She looked at her mother in the mirror.

"Oh child, very good. You look like I did when I was your age." She smiled at her daughter. She took Lexi by her arms and turned her around to face her. "Bobby Ray is a very good looking, very nice young man. He has done so much for us." She shook her head with an appreciative smile. "No matter what you decide, I'll support you."

Giving her mother a look of concern, "Mama, what's that supposed to mean?"

She waved her off. "Nothing. Just know that no matter what,

I'll always be in your corner." Just then, the doorbell rang. "Oh, I bet I know who that is!"

"Shit! I'm not ready!" Lexi rushed to the bathroom to blow dry her hair and do her makeup.

Her mother went downstairs and within a few minutes, she called back up. "It's not him, honey, it's Makayla."

"Have her come on up, Mama!"

"I'm already here," calls a voice from the doorway. Makayla smiled at her friend in the mirror.

Lexi smiled back then turned. "Hey you!" She closed the distance and pulled her friend into an embrace. "What's up?"

"Oh nothing. Just come to see what this happiness is all about from the source herself." Makayla closed the toilet lid and sat down.

"Source of happiness?" She combed out her hair, put some product in it, and began to blow it dry.

"Yeah. Bobby Ray is all giddy like a damn school boy. You have that boy smitten," she laughed.

Lexi grinned. "Well, that's a good thing, isn't it?" She looked at her friend.

"You bet it is." Makayla stood up and approached her friend. "I'm only going to say this once. You hurt him? You deal with me. I love you and you're my best friend, but he's family and he's been through a lot."

"Didn't we have this talk in the beginning? Besides, I'm not going to hurt him." Lexi rolled her eyes. "Besides," she squealed, "I think he's asking me to marry him tonight!"

"Really?" Makayla asked and raised a brow. "I bet you get married before me and Conner."

Lexi blinked then furrowed her brows. "Okay, what's up?"

She shook her head. "It's nothing we can't talk about later. I promise. Tonight is your night, so don't let me spoil it with my negative Nancy shit," she grinned.

"Uh huh. Whatever. Spill." She finished blow-drying her hair and pulled out her flat iron, turning it on. "What happened?"

"Nothing." Makayla sat back down and crossed her arms over her chest.

"Well, something had to have happened."

"No really, NOTHING has happened. He asked me to marry him and now... I can't get him to talk about it." She shrugged then sighed.

"And you've given him ideas on when and where you'd like to have it?" She ran the flat iron through her hair before she moved on to another section.

"Yeah, a few times. *'I don't care, whatever you want'* is what I always get."

"Oh honey, he's a guy. He doesn't care about the planning. You just tell him where to show up and he'll be there. You know, I bet if you tell him to find you at... oh *Billy Bob's* on the mechanical bull, he'd show up, and he'd be ready for a ride!" Both girls laughed.

"Yeah, you're probably right." Makayla stood up and, when Lexi put her iron down, she pulled her into a hug. "I still think there's more to it, but we'll talk about it later. Go get'em." She kissed her cheek. "You look beautiful."

"Aww, thank you, honey!" Makayla left the bathroom just as the doorbell rang again. "Oh shit! I'm still not ready!" She called down to her mother, "Mama! I need like... 15 minutes!"

Her mother called back, "You got it, baby girl!"

Roughly thirty minutes later, Lexi finally came down the stairs in her halter black dress that Robert had fawned over that day. She was also wearing black platform dress shoes with a diamond flower closing the strap, a long red scarf draped over her shoulders, dangling diamond earrings, and her hair down, long and straight.

Robert stood up from the table and his mouth fell open in awe. He stepped closer to her and his eyes moved from hers, down her body, then back up again with a great deal of appreciation. He shook his head then covered his hand with his mouth.

Mrs. Griffin cleared her throat. "I'll give you two a few minutes, but I want pictures before you go."

Lexi answered her without breaking eye contact with him. "Okay Mama." Her mother left the room and the smile on Lexi's lips grew. "So," she turned in a circle. "You like?"

Robert stepped closer and his lips formed a huge smile as he nodded. "I love, I absolutely love, you in this." He leaned in and kissed her cheek then whispered. "Damn baby, you look beautiful." He kissed her cheek again. "I can't wait to get you home." His hands moved to her waist as he pulled her closer.

She closed her eyes and smiled. "We're at my mom's and we have dinner plans first."

"Fuck the plans. I want to take you home," he chuckled.

Lexi pulled back enough to look to his eyes. She smirked. "No baby. We are going to dinner and you will behave or there will be no going home with me in this dress."

He raised his brows. "Well, well. I think I like it when you get demanding."

"More like, in charge." She smirked then quickly kissed him on his lips. Before he could say or do anything else, "Mama! We're ready for our picture!"

Robert reached down and adjusted the hard on in his pants and she giggled. "Yeah, you did that." He winked at her, then turned to face Lexi's mother.

"Say cheese!" Robert wrapped his arm around her waist and pulled her close. The flash lit up and Mrs. Griffin looked at the picture. "Perfect. You may now go forth with the commencing of the shit."

Lexi's eyes widened and she blushed. "Mama!"

"What do you mean, Mrs. Griffin?" He chuckled and knew it had been something said between Lexi and her mother.

"It's nothing!" Lexi pushed him toward the door. "Let's go!"

"No, I want to know!" He laughed. He winked at Mrs. Griffin who in turn, waved, and winked back.

They laughed as they walked out the front door. "Okay, what was that about?" He asked her.

"Really, it's nothing. Don't worry... Oh gosh!" She looked down the driveway and found a limo waiting for them. The driver opened the door for her. "You did this?"

"I sure did." He led her toward the stretch limo and the driver greeted her with a nod.

She smiled and slid into the car. She made room for Robert and waited for him to get in next to her. Once the door closed, she turned to him. "Is there a partition that rolls up, like you see in the movies?"

He grinned. "Mmhmm, sure is."

"Good, because we're using it later," she grinned. "You are so getting lucky later."

Robert chuckled then opened a bottle of champagne. "Here's to many more nights of getting lucky."

"Oh, I'll definitely drink to that."

They drove until they reached Dallas. The limo driver pulled up to Reunion Tower. "Are you serious?" She gasped and looked up at the tall tower. She had heard the floor rotated giving a full view of the city, but she'd never eaten up there.

"Yes, we're eating here." The driver opened the door and Robert stepped out. He offered his hand to Lexi and she accepted, stepping out. She adjusted her scarf around her neck and allowed the long ends to hang down her backside.

They walked inside and Robert pressed the call button for the elevator. He occasionally stole glances at Lexi and smiled. They stepped inside the lift and he pressed the restaurant floor button. As the doors closed, he in turn, closed the distance between them.

Her back pressed against the wall, the cold metal against her bare back. He gently glided his fingers over her cheeks, then cupped her face and kissed her. She moved her hands to his arms and felt his muscles contract. Suddenly, the cold elevator wall wasn't so bad.

The doors chimed and opened. Robert stepped back and wiped off his mouth. He grinned at Lexi and took her hand to lead her inside.

~

*T*hey enjoyed their dinner and the soft music. The floor rotated just as she had heard. At one point, she may have watched the entire city move by in her view. The waitress offered them complimentary dessert. They accepted and she brought out a triple layer chocolate cake with a raspberry filling.

"Lexi," Robert took her hand and ran his thumb over it. "I wrote something for you. Will you allow me to read it?"

She smiled and nodded. "Of course."

He cleared his throat and turned in his chair. He took her hand and kissed the top of it, and looked deep into her eyes. "I love you so much. When I left, it was by far, the hardest time in my life. It helps some, you know, if I write down what I'm feeling." He sighed and continued. "I hope you enjoy it."

Robert's heart beat so hard against his chest for a moment he thought it would explode. He ran his fingers around the corners of his mouth, a nervous habit he picked up a long time ago.

"I'm not one for writing or poetry so I had some help in this. I met with a professor on campus and she helped me put this together. Alright," he sighed and gathered his courage, "I titled this, The One.

Summer romance
That is all it was to be
It all happened so fast
Like a whirlwind
My heart took the leap

And never looked back
You were the one
The first bump in the road I ran away
My heart was shattered
My stubborn pride refused to hear the truth
It wasn't the first time I had been hurt
But God knows, it was the worst
Losing you, I lost myself
You were the one
When I closed my eyes, I envisioned everything with
My days My nights My forever
I will never leave you again
Never doubt this love we share
I want to wake up every morning to your beautiful face
Share every day with you Have a family and grow old with you
My world begins and ends with you
I want you beside me
No matter where this life takes us
An eternity of loving you
Isn't long enough
On my knees, My heart in hand
Lexi Griffin, Will you marry me?"

He dropped down to one knee in front of her and pulled out his small box. Opening the lid, the beautiful diamond blinked under the lights.

Tears slid down her cheeks and she tried to form a smile. Her bottom lip quivered. "Robert..." she whispered his name.

He swallowed hard and waited patiently for her answer.

Lexi finally managed a smile and nodded repeatedly. He stood and pulled her in an embrace. "Yes! I'll marry you, Robert! Yes!"

A roar of claps and cheers erupted in the restaurant. A laugh mixed with tears escaped Lexi's lips as she held onto Robert. He set her down and wiped the tears off her face with his thumbs. He slid the ring onto her finger then looked at it for a moment.

"Oh Robert, it's so beautiful!" Lexi looked over the ring; the princess cut diamond fit perfectly on the bank of smaller princess cut diamonds. She thought the ring was perfect. She looked back into his eyes. "I cannot wait to be your wife."

His forehead pressed gently against hers as he looked into her eyes. "I love you so much. These are the only tears I ever want to see from you, tears of happiness." He tilted his head and kissed her again softly on her lips. "Oh, and in childbirth. I want like twenty kids."

She suddenly turned serious. "Well, I don't think you realize where kids come from mister, because this girl isn't pushing out twenty of your offspring." She laughed. "Make it twenty-one and you have a deal."

He chuckled. "I love you, Lexi." He pulled her in another hug.

"I love you too, baby."

EPILOGUE

*R*obert shut the door to his office and took a seat behind his desk. The voting polls had closed a few hours ago, and the numbers were still coming in. Lexi fell asleep in his office on the couch. He smiled down at her sleeping form and sat down beside her knees.

"Lexi, wake up baby. I have some news."

Her eyes shifted and her lids slowly opened. Her voice was filled with sleep as she yawned. "Robert? What happened? Do you have the results?" She yawned and looked across the room to check the time, finding it was the middle of the night.

"Slow down, darlin'," he told her. "The numbers are still coming in, although the lead does look promising. You might be having an affair tonight with the next Senator of Texas!" He chuckled and leaned into her. He kissed her cheek then pulled her legs onto his lap and relaxed.

"Oh, baby! That's outstanding! I'm so happy for you!"

He smiled and closed his eyes. The stress over the last few months was finally settling down behind him. His fingers absently rotated his wedding band. He tilted his head and looked over to his wedding picture from five years ago. So much had happened in so little time. If it weren't for his stepfather's help, he wasn't sure his campaign would have been successful.

"Baby," she yawned again and with a slight squeal toward the end, "you did it, honey, you did it!"

"I did it with your help, and with Rick's. Without him, I don't think I would have won."

"Now don't talk like that. You did this on your own. Your people listened to you, not to him."

He smiled. "You better be ready for me later tonight, you understand?"

She laughed and shook her head. "Always baby, I'm always ready for you."

~

The next evening, Lexi pulled on a dark blue evening gown that matched the vest in Robert's tuxedo. They were driven out to downtown Dallas to attend the gala to honor his winning the Senate seat. Robert intertwined his fingers with hers, then pulled her hand to his lips and kissed it. "Tonight is only the beginning."

"I'm in no hurry to see the ending," she responded.

"It'll be interesting to see if anyone takes jabs at us again for my political career and you working at the horse track with the gamblers," he chuckled.

She grinned. "Give'em hell, baby."

"Nah, that's your job." He winked then leaned in a kissed her lips.

Stepping out of the limo, flashes of cameras blinded them for a moment then Robert smiled and offered a wave and a few thank you's. Lexi walked by his side as they made their way inside. Many political figures lined the room: the mayors of Dallas, Fort Worth, and Arlington, the Governor and a few judges. Robert shook their hands and thanked them for their vote.

"So who's looking to be the big winner this year, Mrs. Shaw?" One of the judges asked her.

She wasn't sure of his name, but she simply smiled instead. "Oh I can't even begin to tell you that, your honor. You'll have me looking like a gambling fool!" She grinned and winked at the older gentleman. He chuckled and she turned back to Robert.

"Lovely," he grinned.

"What? I can't give away the track secrets."

After dinner, the live band started up and Robert pulled her onto the dance floor. Flashes would occasionally go off from the cameras that captured their dancing. Lexi looked around the room and smiled when she saw Makayla and Conner. She then did a double take at a tattooed young man standing not too far from Makayla's right. "Robert, is that..."

She trailed off and Robert turned to look. "Who let him in here?"

"I have no idea," she responded.

Robert led her off the floor toward Makayla. "I'll be right back, darlin'." He kissed her cheek, nodded to Makayla and Conner, then turned toward the tattooed young man.

"What's going on?" Makayla asked her.

"I'm not sure, but if Blaine's here, something's up," she told her.

"Senator Shaw. Who knew?" Blaine smiled and offered his hand in congratulations.

Robert shook it then gave him a stern look. "Why are you here and how did you get in?"

"My band is quite popular. Didn't take much persuasion. Besides, I'm here to congratulate you and Lexi, nothing more."

"Is that so? I'd say relax and have a good time, but don't blame me for being concerned over what you might do." Robert crossed his arms over his chest and furrowed his brows.

"Ahh now, come on. I wouldn't do that to this nice dinner party. Seems you've done very well for yourself and for Lexi. She deserves happiness. I'm glad she found it with you."

Robert's brows rose. He had no idea what to say to this. "Well, I appreciate that. Thank you." He stood there for a moment then looked back at Lexi. She smiled at him when they made eye contact. Robert winked at her then turned back to Blaine. "Would you like to come say hello?" He regretted it as soon as it was out of his mouth.

"Absolutely. Thank you." Blaine walked past Robert with a smile that stretched ear to ear. Robert's head sank and he sighed, then turned and followed him over. "Lexi Griffin. Damn girl you look good."

She cleared her throat. "It's Shaw now, thank you. Blaine, it's nice to see you doing so well. How's the band?"

"They're great. We're going on a tour soon. I was here for a few days and caught wind of Barbarella's win and thought I'd crash the party."

"Barbarella?" Robert asked him.

"That was supposed to be a joke. Just teasing, man." Blaine playfully slapped Robert's arm. Suddenly, a handful of reporters came over and surrounded them. Between interviewing Robert and finding out Blaine, the lead singer for Deep Ember, was in attendance, the press was having a field day.

Makayla pulled Lexi by her arm, out of the spotlight, to allow the men some face time. "Are you okay with him here?" She asked her.

"Honestly?" Lexi looked between her husband and ex-boyfriend. "It's kind of weird, but at least they're making an effort to get along."

Blaine smiled next to Robert and they shook hands while posing for a picture. He clapped Robert's back once and told him, "Keep in touch."

"Yeah, I'll get right on that," Robert replied with a smirk.

Blaine gave him a quick hug by patting him on the back. "Treat her well or she'll be running back into my arms."

Robert sneered. "I know you'd love that but you need to let

that dream go. It's never going to happen. Now, get out of here before I have you escorted out."

Both men smiled at one another then Blaine turned and began walking out. He stopped and made a beeline for Lexi and Makayla. "Ladies, be good." He leaned in and kissed Makayla on her cheek. She mouthed a few profanities under her breath and wiped the kiss off. He then gently touched Lexi's jawline then leaned in and kissed her cheek. "I'll always love you," he whispered, lowered his head, turned and walked out of the room.

"The nerve!" Makayla shook her head and walked over to Conner, leaning into his embrace.

Robert approached Lexi and tilted her head up. "You okay?"

She nodded. "Yeah, I'm great." She winked at him. "He'll never stop, will he?"

"Probably not. He'll always want what he can't have."

"Maybe if Abby played a little hard to get, he'd be with her right now, instead."

"Maybe," Robert said.

"Well, she seems to be doing fine so I wouldn't pass him off on her, either." She grinned then stood on her toes and kissed him. "I love you, my Senator." She giggled.

"Mmm, I love you, too." He leaned in and whispered to her, "Rather than calling me god tonight, how about you scream out Senator? Fuck me, Senator?"

Lexi felt her face blush crimson. "I cannot believe you just went there!" She shook her head and laughed. She pulled him back down to her ear level. "Only if you dance with me first—to some Joe Cocker!"

"You will never let me live that down, will you?" He chuckled.

"Absolutely not!"

THE END

Check out the next story in the Southern Roots series, City Lights!
Here's Chapter One!

I don't like being out of control. I don't like not having everything around me... my way. Addiction... that's what they say I have. They tell me it'll all be okay. They tell me that soon, this too shall pass. What the fuck does that even mean?
Lexi left me. She was my life before my music career. I fucked her over, fucked my bandmates over... might as well hand over my contract to Chuck, my manager.
"Kid, you royally fucked up," he told me. He stood there, shaking his head like I should have known better.
"Don't fucking judge me, you fat prick! You have no idea what I've been through. You have no idea how this fucking feels."
Of course, this was one month into rehab. This was the morning I finally got out of bed, made my way to the bathroom, and found a stranger looking at me in the mirror. His eyes were sunken in and bloodshot. With his shaven head, honestly, he looked strung out. Who the fuck was this person?
Oh right, that's me. They told me this would not be fun. They told me I needed to clean up and get sober.
"The amount of drugs we found in your system... Blaine, it's a miracle you didn't overdose permanently," the doctor told me. What the hell does he know? He's here to treat me. He knows nothing of addiction.
I bent over and grabbed the sink when my stomach suddenly lurched. Dry heaving first thing in the morning is something I'm used to. After an all-night binge fest on coke, ecstasy, and more liquor than I could hold... repercussions usually met up with me the next day.
Having rinsed out my mouth, the water dripped from my chin back into the sink. Small little fingers danced their way up my

back, to my shoulders. They latched on and a faint whisper sounded in my ear.

Make the call. They'll bring you something, the voice told me.

My conscience enjoyed mind fucking me from time to time. "No," I told myself. My head began to pound and sweat beaded on my brow. I retched again then fell to my knees. I coughed a few times and memories of Lexi, my mom, and the band all hovered over me.

Blaine, stop it, please.

Why are you doing this? What happened?

Where did this come from? Who gave you this?

What did I ever do to deserve this from you? I'm your mother, for Christ's sake!

All these voices in my head fuck with me as my mind whispers its wants and needs. Just one more hit. Just one. One won't hurt me. It'll take the edge off.

I crept along the floor toward the bathroom door. My fingers barely wrapped around the edge of it and I pulled it open. My orderly stood outside, keeping some sort of guard. Guard of what? Who the hell knows?

"Help…" my voice was soft and it sounded rough. He looked down… all 250 pounds of former wrestler… maybe football player… turned orderly. He shot up an eyebrow and stared me down.

"Feeling better there, Mister Rock Star?" He squatted down and his brown eyes bore into mine. This man, whose tag read Stanley, obviously gave no fucks about me, if the smirk on his lips was any evidence of that anyway. "I see your kind here day in and day out. Poor little rock star got his feelings hurt so he turned to drugs. Did someone hurt you before, Blaine, or are you lashing out at your upbringing? Did mommy and daddy mistreat you?"

"Fuck you!" I managed to mumble out.

"Ahh, so he lives." Stanley stood and shook his head. "Are you thinking, maybe, of trying to escape? Tell you what," he looked up and down the hall way for a moment then turned his attention back to me. He bent over and grabbed my shoulders, hauling me to my feet. He wasn't gentle about it and if I wasn't so fucked up on coming clean, I'd have fucking punched his nose in. "I'll help you escape and get some dope IF..." he trailed off with that same smirk, "you can get past me." He tossed me back into my bathroom. My back hit the sink and I fell onto my ass, hard. "What the fuck, man?" I rubbed my back and stared up at the orderly. I sighed and watched as he crossed his thick arms over his chest. He's fucking with me. He's mind fucking me. Hell, he's probably in my mind right now doing this.

I looked away from the man named Stanley and laid down on my side, the cool tile chilling my sweaty body. The odd thing about going through withdrawal is the overly hot feeling your body gains during the process... but the cold chills. It's like having the flu. You're cold and shivering, yet you have a temperature. Stanley turned and left my vision, probably standing guard outside my door. How did I afford such luxury? Oh yeah, I'm a rock star.

I pulled myself to my hands and knees and made my way back into my bedroom. I crawled up onto my bed to lie down. I stared at the white walls that surrounded me. Each time I closed my eyes, the nightmare that is my life invaded my mind. If I kept my eyes open, I began to see shit that wasn't there.

Isn't there something they can give me? Like a sedative? Oh yeah, they can't. I'm in rehab.

I can recall exactly when this started for me. It was my third big show. I barely made it to the end on fumes. We had a show the following night and I was completely exhausted. The band we were opening for, their lead singer... what's his name... offered me coke. I could kick him in the fucking nuts now.

Soon, it was ecstasy for the ride it gave. Sometimes, it was acid for the trips. After the shows, we drank until we couldn't see. I had women at my disposal. I never slept alone. I would close my eyes and if I were just sober enough, Lexi would be in my vision. So I drank more. I smoked more. I snorted more.

Something wet touched my pillow but it wasn't sweat. I hadn't cried since I was a child. The pain I put my family through, Lexi and her mother… especially after her father died. And now my band. Why did I do this? Oh yeah, because I'm an asshole, mother-fucker who only thinks of himself.

Well, that changes now. No longer will I allow the demons to control my every move. No longer will I allow anyone around me who uses. No longer will I allow any of this to control me. Never again.

But just one more time won't hurt you.

Fuck you, coke demons. Fuck you.

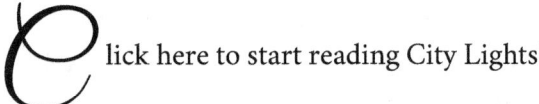lick here to start reading City Lights!

Ainsley sits down with Chase's most expensive scotch in one hand and fancy pen in the other and pours it all out, literally and figuratively. When Chase finds the note—and a passed-out Ainsley—he's intrigued. Perhaps there's more to the soft-spoken Ms. Speire than he thought.

Ainsley wakes to Chase's trademark cocky grin, and Chase sees a new spark in Ainsley's eyes. Anything between them would be an HR nightmare, but is there a chance Chase and Ainsley are willing to work together on one more case? A case that promises a lifetime sentence of love?

Read these stories in KU!

Southern Roots series

Southern Roots

City Lights

Fueled Desire

Driven Hunger

Paramour

Playing Her Body

Suspenseful Seduction World

Submitting to Paradise

Claiming His Snow

Hot SEALs

Guarded by a SEAL

Available wide!

Special Ops series

Delta Force

Sniper

Misadventures series

Misadventures with a Firefighter

Misadventures with a Lawyer

ABOUT THE AUTHOR

USA TODAY and Award-winning Bestselling Author, Julie Morgan (writing as J. Morgan), holds a degree in Computer Science and loves science fiction shows and movies. Encouraged by her family, she began writing. Originally from Texas, Julie now resides in Central Florida with her husband and daughter where she is an advocate for Special Needs children and can be found playing games with her daughter when she isn't lost in another world.

Keep up with Julie. Join her newsletter and receive a free book!
www.juliemorganbooks.com/newsletter.html
julie@juliemorganbooks.com

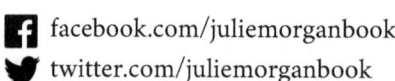

facebook.com/juliemorganbook
twitter.com/juliemorganbook
instagram.com/JulieMorganBooks